FORBIDDEN

Nat had his work to absorb him. She had to go
back to a husband she loathed. And she
wasn't the type to enjoy pretence and
deception. Nat had little or no conscience about
Guy. He was a sadist. A man who had enjoyed
destroying his young wife's innocence . . . She
was one of his valuable possessions — like
the paintings he collected

Forbidden

Denise Robins

CORONET BOOKS
Hodder Paperbacks Ltd., London

Copyright © 1971 by Denise Robins

First published by Hodder & Stoughton
Ltd. in 1971

Coronet edition 1973
Fourth impression 1982

———————————————————

Printed and bound in Great Britain for
Hodder and Stoughton Paperbacks, a
division of Hodder and Stoughton Ltd.,
Mill Road, Dunton Green, Sevenoaks,
Kent (Editorial Office: 47 Bedford
Square, London, WC1 3DP) by
Cox & Wyman Ltd, Reading

ISBN 0 340 17408 0

I

They neither of them knew the way, but the driver was being briefed by the woman at his side, reading from a letter.

"Once you reach the village of Mougins drive straight through, past the little fountain in the Square, and then down the hill until you come to a sign that says '*Mas Candille*'— your hotel—where you turn left."

They had reached the Square. Nat pulled in under a sheltering tree.

"Let's get out and have a nice cold drink in that little place on our left. What's it called? *Hotel de la France*. It looks charming and I'm damn thirsty."

"That goes for two of us," said Toni.

They were both hot and drenched with perspiration. It was eighty-five degrees today and no wind. They had driven three hundred kilometres from Avignon, having put the car on the train at Boulogne and spent the night in the *wagon-lit*. An admirable way of skidding over the miles and waking up to the sunlight of Provence.

Oh, thought Toni, *this beautiful warm Provençal sunshine. It does something to you. It made you feel better at once. You glow—blissful, glad to be alive. Certainly not as they had both been feeling back in England. But that was another story.*

"The Triumph has done us well," said Nat Olver as he got out and examined his dusty five-year-old car. The fond look of an indulgent parent.

Toni said:

"Well, you always take good care of it. But you take good

5

care of everything," she added, and held out her hand. He squeezed it. With an arm around her shoulders, he walked to the welcome green gloom of the little restaurant where tables were laid under thick vines and there were trees to keep away the blistering sun. A waitress took their order. Iced beer for Nat; lager for Toni.

They could sit in the cool facing the Square and watch the diamond brightness of the fountain splashing into a round stone basin. The village seemed deserted except for an old woman in black, waddling along with two long loaves tucked under her arm; and a young man who mounted his motor bike, and roared off disturbing the peace of the late afternoon.

They could also see an apricot-coloured house with the word "*Mairie*" written over it and a low-windowed antique shop with paintings and pieces of pottery displayed outside.

The sky was a clear blue. The sharp contrast between sunlit walls and shadowed alleys was strikingly beautiful. It was a place for artists.

"Oh," said Toni, "I'm glad we chose to come here."

"So am I," said Nat, "It looks enchanting."

"I must buy a postcard and send it to Chris."

"Women always seem to enjoy sending postcards."

"Will it irritate you if I write cards?" she asked.

Now his smile vanished. Nat had a lean rather serious face with hollows under the cheek bones, and blue narrow eyes. Still in his early thirties he looked young in his sports shirt, linen jeans and with an untidy mop of dark brown hair. Ordinarily, Toni remembered, he was a smart, West End doctor, rather careful of his appearance. She preferred him as he was today. She loved him more than anything on earth.

"Why should I be irritated by anything you do?" he asked. "But I don't quite see who you're going to send cards to except Chris who is the only one who *knows* about us."

Her enthusiasm over the local postcards she generally sent on holiday evaporated. Of course, she knew she had been

6

stupid about that. She could not send any—except to Chris. All her relatives and friends believed that she was with Chris and Joe—in Ireland, where they were on holiday.

Toni felt half ashamed that she had had to go to such lengths to make her story water-tight. She had written a letter to Guy her husband for Chris to post from Connemara. And she had left a card to be sent to Mrs. Millins, her house-keeper, who looked after her country house in Bray.

"You're so right," she said. "Nobody else must know we are here."

"I couldn't bear anything to spoil your ten days with me."

"Nothing will. Nothing could."

Under the table his warm hand pressed one of her bare knees. Toni—christened Antonia—was a striking-looking girl. Not classically beautiful—her nose was too short and her mouth too wide, but she had the sort of childish face with small chin, wide brow and smooth creamy complexion which most men found attractive and endearing. Nat had at first thought her still a teenager and been amazed to find that she was twenty-four and married. As for her eyes—he felt that he had drowned in Toni's eyes from the very first moment he met her; and a fatal moment it had proved for both of them. Nat knew from the start that it wasn't too good for a man in his profession to get involved with a married woman. He was and had been a dedicated surgeon since he left the big London hospital where he had qualified and later added the F.R.C.S. to his name.

Toni's eyes were remarkable—more golden than hazel. Her long dark hair curved smoothly to her shoulders. On first meeting he had found her warm and friendly. He had gone home from the party remembering her. She was strangely immature for a married woman, even shy.

On further acquaintance he had discovered that she had been badly hurt by life. She hardly mentioned her husband and she was not at all the ordinary rich girl who marries money.

Yet she was wearing a ring with one of the biggest emeralds he had ever seen.

It was not until later that he had found out that she hated that ring and regarded it as a badge of slavery, but because her husband wanted her to show it off, and to avoid argument, she had given in.

Now Nat knew so much more about her.

Normally, he had excellent health and had never really been ill. But during these last couple of months—ever since he realised that he was desperately in love with Toni—he had felt off-colour and nervy, and lost nearly half a stone. He was a man who always attracted women. He had had minor affairs. But with his mind and heart set on his profession—the hospital, and his gynaecology taking up most of his time and energy, he had so far avoided marriage.

He removed his hand from Toni's knee and said abruptly:

"This all seems unreal. How come we are just about to check in at an hotel in Mougins as Mr. and Mrs. Gray?"

"I don't know. It seems pretty unreal to me, too—but wonderful."

"I don't mind for myself, but it does rather weigh on my conscience that *you* are taking such a frightful risk, Toni."

"The risk's greater for you. You're a surgeon—a well-known gynaecologist."

"Even if we were found out they couldn't strike me off, because you're not my patient."

"But a scandal wouldn't do you any good," she cut in, and drained the cool foaming liquid from her glass. Then she shook her head. "Nat, Nat, why did it have to happen this way? Why didn't we meet before?"

"That's the sixty-four-thousand-dollar question, my love."

"The right people never seem to meet in time, if at all."

Nat fixed his eyes on the glittering fountain.

"I know. My mother was very unhappy," Toni added.

"Poor sweet. My own parents met and married at the right

time. They loved each other till the end. But things were always difficult for my mother. She was half-Jewish, you know. I was christened Nathaniel after her father who was in fact a Rabbi. But my own father was one hundred per cent Gentile. He ran a small radio and T.V. business in London. They were always either broke or flourishing. Finally Mother had to go out to work. Eventually she ran a dress-shop. Then the war came. Father sold his business and joined up. He was rather a splendid fellow. I got a scholarship, and a small legacy from my Jewish grandfather which just about covered my years of training in medicine. Incidentally, my Rabbi grandfather died in Dachau—just one more victim of the Nazis."

Toni looked at him with passion and tenderness.

"I adore that touch of Jew in you—it's given you brains as well as subtlety. I think the Jewish people are so artistic and sensitive."

He laughed and ordered two more drinks.

"It's pleasant here. Let's go on drinking and talking. I'm just beginning to cool off, aren't you?"

"Yes. And remembering what you've said about the dangers we're facing—I really don't think you need worry about us being here. Darling Chris will cover up for us."

"She's a good friend to you, Toni."

"We were terrifically friendly at school. We were in Switzerland together. Joe is an accountant. They have a flat in Ovington Gardens. You like my Chris, don't you, Nat?"

"She's very nice indeed—but without your attractions."

"I think she's very sweet to look at," said Toni loyally, "and she sort of radiates good humour, she's so happy. She adores her husband and they have the sweetest baby boy."

He sat silent, smoking, relaxed. Then she said:

"Listen, darling, before we go any further I want to make sure you believe as I do that there *is* no real danger. I mean for you. I've really reached a point where I couldn't care less if Guy divorced me tomorrow—I hate him so much."

9

"You're angelic. I hate to think of you living with Guy. It's an insult to any woman to be forced to go to bed with a man she feels that way about."

"Please don't think about it today."

"And you're sure *he* won't be back in London until the week after *we* get back?"

"Sure. He's definitely gone to Rio. I saw him off. I've had orders to take the Rolls and chauffeur down to Heathrow and meet him when he comes back. I've already got the date and the flight number. You know—I've always told you—Guy is the most meticulous person. He rarely changes his mind. He isn't likely to come back until the day he said he will. Besides—this South American trip is important to him. His firm is insuring the building of a huge dam somewhere out there and it will be worth millions. Money—money—ugh! I hate it—"

"You're an amazing girl. Dollars seem to mean nothing to you."

"Neither do jewels. It's marvellous for me to be wearing none," and she held out her slender ringless hands with satisfaction.

He wished—as he had been doing ever since he fell in love with Toni—that he was not a well-known surgeon, and that he could have just taken her away altogether and given her the happiness she wanted. So far he had been entirely absorbed in his profession. He had a large private practice. He shared a consulting room with a colleague—a heart-specialist—Keith Lucas-Wright. Nat could hardly forget all these things, much as he desired Toni.

He looked at her rather enviously—she seemed so blissfully happy—living for the moment. Women are capable of that—so much more than men are, he decided.

"Oh, darling," said Toni, "I can't think of anything except the fact that we're going to be together as Mr. and Mrs. Gray for a whole ten days—alone, day and night. Won't it be gorgeous?"

He nodded, smiling. They had chosen the name *Gray* because it had been her mother's maiden name. As he paid the bill and they drove away, Nat remembered the first night he had ever spent with Toni.

Guy was away on business in Paris. Nat had dined with Toni in their penthouse—in a huge block facing the river. There were no servants to spy. It was a service-flat. It had seemed to the lovers quite safe. But the small risk they ran, nevertheless, spoilt some of the rapture.

During the last two months, there had been other meetings —equally unsatisfactory and nerve-racking. Nat had his work to absorb him. She had to go back to a husband she loathed. And she wasn't the type to enjoy pretence and deception. Nat had little or no conscience about Guy. He was a sadist. A man who had enjoyed destroying his young wife's innocence. He treated her without tenderness or understanding. She was one of his valuable possessions—like the paintings he collected. Nat's concern for Toni made the position almost unbearable. But when at last his feelings ran away with him and he said "to hell—let's get a divorce", Toni stoutly refused to agree—for his sake. And she never wavered from that.

One of her chief attractions for Nat was the fascinating mixture of strength and weakness in her character, and the strong side dominated.

*   *   *

Once they reached *Mas Candille*—the hotel Chris had chosen for them—Nat doggedly turned his back on all their problems.

The small hotel was enchanting. Once a private house, it was built of stone, and half-covered in flowering creepers. Three tall trees stood at intervals flatly against the façade, like green sentries stiffly on guard. There were white painted chairs and tables on a broad terrace under white umbrellas from which there was one of the most beautiful views in the district. One looked far up the misty mountain side toward Grasse or down the valley in the direction of the sea.

Everywhere there were big tubs of vivid flowers. In the restaurant one incredible tree, looking as though it had grown out of the stones, was a solid mass of exotic pink blossom.

The *patron* and his wife were charming. M. et Mme. Gray were given just the sort of room they wanted. At the back of the hotel, their french windows opened on one side out into a garden. They could walk up a few steps, then a path to the small swimming pool. The room was spacious and essentially French with bare polished wood floor and antique furniture. A heavy carved wood chest of drawers, a painted cupboard, and a wide double bed with a white quilt. There was an atmosphere of tranquillity, simplicity and peace—all they had longed for and never been able to find in London.

After Nat had parked his car and the young waiter who had brought in their cases departed and closed the door behind him, Nat went to the windows at the further end of the bedroom and pushed open the shutters. In the heat of the day they were shut. It kept the room cool and dim. But with the Englishman's essential longing for the sun, Nat felt compelled to let its warmth pour upon him. It was a truly beautiful view. The sky was incredibly blue and pure. Far below he could just see the white curve of the Auto-route leading to Nice.

Nat pulled the damp shirt over his head, flung it on the floor and threaded his fingers through his thick dark hair.

"God, it's hot, I must have a bath."

Toni examined the bathroom with feminine appreciation. "It's sweet—so clean and shining."

"Sweet," he echoed, jeering, "What a description of a bathroom."

She giggled.

"I'll run a bath for you, doctor."

"Don't call me that," he said suddenly, jerkily, "I don't want to be reminded of it or anything back home."

"Nor do I," she breathed and ran to him, and pressed her cheek against his naked chest, brushing the brown curling hair with her lips. "Monsieur Gray," she whispered, "it seemed so funny to hear them call me *Madame* Gray."

His arms enfolded her; with his right one he gently pulled down the zip of her cotton frock and began to push the dress off her bare shoulders. As it fell at her feet he pressed his lips to her long throat.

"Don't let's start having a conscience about anything. It's too late," he said and pressed her whole body against his.

She felt his strong heart-beats against her breast. Suddenly she came alive, tingling from head to foot. When she opened her eyes he thought he had never seen anything more beautiful, they were so large, so expressive of her roused passion. He knew that she wanted him as much as he wanted her. He let her go for a moment, walked to the windows and drew the shutters together again, reducing the room to its former cool darkness. With his lips fiercely demanding upon hers, he pulled her to the big white bed.

2

In the night Toni woke up. For a moment she did not know where she was. She thought she must be back in her own Empire bed—the splendid one Guy had bought for her in Paris—a magnificent affair with taffeta-silk ribbons sweeping from all four posts, and a fabulous white lace spread.

Soon she realised that she was in quite a different kind of bed and that the man who lay beside her was not her husband. She put out a hand and touched his back; a thin rather bony back. She loved it.

He turned over and took her in his arms.

"Darling—my darling!"

She ran her fingers through his hair and kissed him with hungry passion.

After a moment she drew away, sat up and switched on the table lamp. Nat reached for a packet of cigarettes. He said:

"You'll have all the mosquitoes in with that light on, my love. I'll close the shutters."

"It'll be hot, but I don't care."

"Let's just look at each other for a moment. I like to see your face."

"I like to see yours. No—no cigarette," she added.

"I need one to calm my nerves," Nat grinned at her, and struck a match. She gazed at him speculatively and with admiration. He could be so many different people. The clever formal consultant—fast making a name for himself; or the ordinary human being, like this one tonight. A man of deep understanding. A perfect lover. She had never guessed a man could be so fiercely passionate yet so tender.

"I love you," she said and wondered how many times she had uttered those words.

He put an arm around her. They leaned their heads back against the pillows. The room was full of the strange odour of a green pastille burning, in a spiral, on their dressing table. A 'contraption' as Nat called it, given to them by the manager. He claimed that the special vapour kept away all winged insects. True enough, they had not yet been disturbed by the whine of one mosquito.

"Isn't it fun here?" Toni spoke dreamily.

"Much more than that," he said, "Toni, we're both so wide awake, tell me about yourself. More than you've ever told me. You've only sort of sketched your past life for me because we've so far had such hideously curtailed times together. As soon as we've begun to learn intimate facts about each other, it's been time to go—and farewell!"

"I know," she sighed, "I've often wanted to tell you things I've never told you, and to hear more about *you*. Then we could feel closer. Why must tonight ever end, Nat? Oh, why is it only going to be ten short days for us?"

"It's all life offers. Remember your Omar Khayyam? *'One moment in annihilation's waste'?*"

She nodded and sighed.

"Your life hasn't been wasted, darling Nat. You do a great service to humanity. It's my life that's been a complete wash-out."

"I don't like to hear you say that."

"But it's true—"

"Look, Toni, why don't you come away with me and let everything else go—?" he began.

"Darling, not again," she protested. "You must believe me when I tell you that Guy is a horribly vindictive person and if I left him for you, he'd use all the money he's got to try and hurt you."

"Damn and blast Guy," said Nat under his breath, "I've never met him but I loathe his guts."

She shuddered and hung on to Nat tightly.

"So do I. *So do I.*"

"Listen, my love, you've been through a lot you've never even told me about. Here we are, shut away from the world. Tell me everything, right from the start. Get the horrors out of your subconscious."

"I don't really want to spoil tonight by talking about *him.*"

"It'll never stop festering deep down inside you, my love, unless you do bring it out. This is a good quiet time—tell me all."

"All?" she sighed.

"Yes—we'll record your autobiography like this together."

"Okay," said Toni suddenly, "I'll smoke after all. Light a cigarette for me. I'll start—right from when I was small. Sometimes I admit it kills me to realise that most people look on me now as a pampered puss with an adoring millionaire husband. In public, Guy seems so kind and devoted. In private he's horrible. He's schizophrenic."

"Start from your childhood, darling," Nat interrupted, softly.

"Okay. Everything was fine until my mother died. She was pretty, sweet and gay. One of two sisters. But not like my Aunt Penelope, who I had to live with eventually; she was always a sourpuss and has never married. Poor Mummy was brave as well as beautiful. She hid her troubles behind her gaiety. She worshipped my father and he broke her heart."

Nat's hold around Toni's waist tightened.

"Like mother—like daughter—you've hidden your sorrows very well."

"Well, Daddy was not as bad a man as Guy. He was just too keen on women. But he was lovable and Mummy forgave him even when she found out that he was unfaithful. The last straw came when she discovered she had cancer and knew she

16

couldn't live. She was terribly ill and being nursed at home. Daddy made a pass at her nurse. I was fifteen. I saw for myself what was happening. Then the nurse, who was pretty and silly but a decent girl, actually came to me and said she was sorry but she couldn't stay because of my father. So we got a new nurse. One evening I was talking to Mummy, trying to make up a good story as to why the other nurse left, Mummy opened those wonderful eyes of hers and said: 'You needn't try to spare me, darling. *I know.* I've always known.' When I cried, she comforted me and said that she wasn't upset any more and that, after all, Daddy was good-looking and vigorous and she had been so ill and he needed some fun and so on. Daddy, as usual, was marvellous to her in between his love affairs and during the last month of her life he never left her bedside, so she died happily enough."

Nat drew a long sigh.

"And you, my poor love, just a child—were left to yourself; lonely and disillusioned in men right from the start."

"Let's turn over the record," she said with a brief laugh, "We'll skip those awful days after Mummy's funeral. Then came Daddy's second marriage—only three months later, to a young Australian girl—the opposite of Mummy. Only about five years older than me. Rather good-looking but a bit loud, and rather sexy in her blatant way. I didn't blame Daddy. I didn't even feel resentful because of Mummy. I just crept into my shell—a sort of ivory tower I had built around myself— and I don't think I even shed a tear when I saw Daddy and Bunny—that's what he called her—off to Sydney. Daddy settled there. He was a chartered accountant. I think I once told you. He got a job at once in Sydney.

"Bunny's father was a wealthy grain-broker and she had plenty of money of her own. They wanted to take me with them but nothing would induce me to go. I didn't really care for Daddy once I found out about that nurse. He arranged for me to live with Aunt Penny in London. She was and is still a bit eccentric and couldn't have been more unlike Mummy in looks or character. She ran an antique shop; still runs it, in Hampstead. It's fairly successful. She told Daddy she'd be glad to have me live with her when I left my Swiss school. I might help her in the shop, etc. So began the second phase of my life. I survived constant battles between my aunt and myself. I didn't give way easily, shy and reserved though people find me. I fought Aunt Penny but hated her whole outlook on life. She was interested in the antiques only because of the commercial value. I was only interested in beauty—in art—in romance. And the sort of friendly warm atmosphere that was lacking in her home. I soon found out that she only really took me on because Daddy left her some money for the continuation of my education—and my keep.

"Anyhow, my aunt was always calling me ungrateful and saying how like Mummy I was and that she'd always thought Mummy stupid. I felt I just couldn't work in her shop and be tied to her day *and* night. I made up my mind to get away and strike out on my own. I was nearly eighteen when I came back from Vevey. I could speak and write good French, and after a blistering row one day, Aunt Penny and I parted company. I found a job with a family in Paris through the Contactus Agency who placed *au-pair* girls. I taught English to the two children of a French diplomat. I was quite happy for a few months. The family were very nice to me and I liked my two pupils. Then one night—oh, Nat, I can't tell you what fate had in store for me—Madame gave a big buffet supper party for a lot of her husband's diplomatic friends. Monsieur also had strong interests in a French insurance company owned by his brother, and it so happened that his brother was a close friend of Guy's. Guy, you know, inherited a fortune, and was continuing to make more despite taxation. His firm, Brand and Skipperton, insure vast enterprises such as the construction of dams and bridges in all parts of the world. He gets huge contracts. He's a brilliant man in his way."

"So you met him at this supper party in Paris?" said Nat.

"Yes."

"Describe him."

"He is most peculiar. Monsieur was impressed by his brains and Madame, who had met him, by his outward charm. When I first saw him I thought him terrific—poor innocent that I was! Elegant. Faultlessly cut suit; perfect shirt; tie from Sulka (he used to buy at least a dozen every time he came to Paris); hand-made shoes. He's what Madame calls *très distingué*. He was about thirty then but running to fat. He's a great gourmet and drinks the best wines. But with good tailoring he manages to conceal his bad figure. Like so many men of his build, he walks lightly and dances well. We danced together later that night of the party. He showed me what a Viennese waltz could really be. His face—" Nat felt her shudder suddenly, "I dislike him so much now that I can hardly describe him without prejudice. But you can see his prototype on certain Roman statues—full-lidded eyes, as cold and grey as the Northern sea, short curly hair. His is reddish-gold and he has a chin with a cleft in it. Handsome; but he shows all his teeth when he laughs and can twist his lips into a horrid little circle. It's a cruel mean mouth."

"Go on, darling," said Nat and his fingers stroked her bare shoulder which he kissed now and again.

"He smiled at me delightfully when I was introduced to him by Madame and bent over my hand with Continental courtesy. He is always courteous even if he's doing or saying something horrible. That's the worst of Guy. It's like living with a polite robot. And not a very nice one. Then there were his hands. They're cruel, too, plump and soft. He has his nails regularly manicured. But I didn't pay much attention to such details then. As you can imagine, I was a young girl and an employee and rather dazzled because I had been permitted to join the guests. Madame said she thought it time I got to know some nice young men though one couldn't exactly call Guy Brand a

nice young man! On the contrary, he was very sophisticated—
a man of the world. Well, he smiled down at me with those
extraordinary cold eyes. I was fascinated. He kept looking at
me. I was eighteen then, and had few nice clothes but
Madame who was quite slim for her age had dressed me up in
one of her own cast-offs. White pleated chiffon with a jewelled
collar. Rather super. It came from one of the *haute couture*
salons in Rome. Madame used to buy a lot of her clothes
from Balenciaga.

"During dinner, sitting next to Guy, I found him a brilliant
conversationalist. It was all above my head, but he made me
talk about myself and seemed interested, and I heard about his
penthouse, his business and his hobbies. Although, of course,
I knew a bit. Madame had already told me he had a famous
and very fine collection of Old Masters.

"He took me out to dinner that next day and at the end of it
said he must see me again. I can actually remember his words:
'Antonia'—he never used my nickname—'I'm a perfectionist.
Everything I have must be perfect. *You* are perfect and I admire
you tremendously.' I didn't of course realise the implication of
those words.

"The next time we met in Paris he asked me to marry him.
Naturally at eighteen, I was dazzled and flattered because he
had always been considered by Paris Society to be so very
eligible and he was so charming to me *then*. Monsieur and
Madame encouraged the whole affair."

"And so?" Nat questioned.

"So I fell for it and said 'yes'. One of those things that
seemed to attract him so much was the fact that I had never
slept with anybody. He wanted to be the first."

In the darkness and silence of the summer's night, she felt
Nat's distaste for this and she embraced him convulsively.

"If only *you* had been first, Nat. I would like to have given
you everything—*everything*, darling."

"Don't let's lose our sense of proportion, my sweet," he

20

tried to cover up his own tension. "Carry on. Guy proposed. You accepted and you got married. Where?"

"In Paris. Incidentally, because I was under age—they hadn't brought in the new law then—we had to get my aunt's permission. She gave it only too willingly. We hadn't corresponded since I went to France but she was quite willing to welcome me again once she heard about the great Guy. I think she hoped he'd buy all her antiques! But you can imagine her potty little things never attracted *him*. And he hadn't the kind of nature that would allow him to go and buy her rubbish just to help a stupid woman. *You* would have done that.

"Well, we were married on a cold wet day in Paris. I was not a white bride. We were not married in a church, either, because Guy was not at all a religious man. I wore a fabulous honey-coloured dress and jacket trimmed with sable— a Balmain—one of the first of a new collection. Guy told Madame to get me the sort of trousseau she would buy for one of her own girls. What with the model dresses and gorgeous Italian shoes and bags, and a sable jacket (which must have cost Guy thousands), I had a trunk-full quite fit for a millionaire's wife. I began to feel suffocated, even scared. And the night before the wedding I had awful qualms about really loving Guy and wanting to go to bed with him. Perhaps I had a hunch that there was something I wouldn't like behind all that charm. But I told myself I was being stupid and fooled myself into believing I still wanted to marry him.

"We should have gone to Nassau for our honeymoon but an emergency business deal in Mexico cropped up for Guy, so we flew off to London after our reception. Guy had to pick up some important documents from his office, then book our passage to Mexico City. He arranged for us to spend our first night in his penthouse. And then. . . ."

She paused. Nat felt that her silence in some way thickened the atmosphere. It grew sinister with the memories she was reviving. Almost he laid a hand across her lips and told her to say no more. But he kept quiet.

After it was all over, he believed that he could share and lessen her suffering, and her grief.

"I remember," she said, "Guy had ordered wonderful flowers. It was all fabulously luxurious in the flat. Champagne and caviar were served. There were soft lights and sweet music—the lot—very romantic. I was impressed.

"When he came to bed he made love to me—very quickly—and it was my first disillusionment. He was ghastly. After which he never slept with me normally again. I discovered that he was not interested, as ordinary men are, in sex. He was icily sensual in a peculiar way. He *froze* me, Nat. His whole attitude disgusted me. I had gone to my marriage with a young girl's idea of passionate, shared love and tenderness."

Nat's hand gripped one of hers convulsively.

"Bloody awful for you," he whispered.

"Mind you, I was far from ignorant and not at all prudish. I had frankly looked forward to marriage, but Guy frightened me. I realised from the start that he was a sort of sadist. Soon after our marriage he developed this terrific desire to turn me into a valuable possession. A desire that had little to do with the natural love of a husband for his wife. It was kind of peculiar. During our honeymoon, for instance, he continually made me undress and then insisted on decking me out with jewels. Like that I had to pose, while he painted me in the nude. I hated it. He had quite a talent for painting, actually. In his way Guy is an artist; but with an absolute lack of sensibility—any understanding of a woman's feeling. A lot of the things he made me do embarrassed and upset me. When I *didn't* do what he wanted he was furious and quite often cruel. If I cried he'd tell me I must learn self-control. As far as normal love-making was concerned, I quickly stopped wanting it and began to hate him both physically and mentally."

"He sounds charming," muttered Nat, deeply disgusted.

"You can't break through to a person like Guy. He never seems to be able to communicate. I heard from a cousin of his one day that he was strange even as a boy. He was cruel to animals. But the way he behaved *before* our marriage entirely misled me. Our marriage was never warm or friendly. Imagine, Nat, as time passed what an effect this all had on me!"

"Poor child!"

"Mind you, I've been a coward," added Toni, "I could have walked out. I've often wanted to. But he's so cunning. Once or twice when I was driven to screaming point he seemed afraid I'd run away and begged me not to leave him. He asked me to forgive his oddness and so on. You know, Nat— as Mrs. Guy Brand I was one of the great successes in his life. Wherever we went, London, Paris or New York, I was admired (though God knows why), and it seemed to give him a colossal kick. Nat, I was always desperately lonely. But I sat back— rather weakly, I suppose. *Until I met you.*"

Nat lit another cigarette. He needed it.

"Oh, God!" he groaned. "What a stinking awful show!"

She stroked his head.

"But I'm okay now, my darling, because I did find you and I must be able to meet you sometimes in the future. I can never let you go right out of my life. When we can't meet. . . . What was it some poet said? . . . '*I will wear your love like a cloak and it will shelter me from the cruel cold world*' . . . Oh, Nat, I love you so much. Hold me—kiss me!"

They made love feverishly, filled with a despairing passion that drew them yet closer together.

The night wore on. They did not sleep again.

Finally, the dawn-light filtered through the closed shutters.

Nat got up, opened the jalousies and looked over the misty valley toward the gold-rimmed mountains. It was a fresh, beautiful, inspiring morning. He felt in need of mental rehabilitation after listening to Toni's story. And God alone knew what *she* must need, poor sweet, he thought.

He turned and saw her sitting up in bed, her arms folded across her bare breasts, her long dark hair tumbled, half-veiling her face. She looked, he thought, like a sad Niobe, weeping, grieving over her ruined life—a life in which the sable coats, the diamonds, and the playgrounds of millionaires, could not compensate her.

For himself there seemed little ahead but emptiness outside his work. But even this which used to mean so much, seemed to have lost its full magnetism. He knew he'd get it all back in time. The moment he was with a new patient, he always became deeply interested and involved. And no doubt he *would* be able to meet poor little Toni from time to time—that was if her damned husband didn't catch on to the fact that she was having 'an affair'. God knows what he might not do if he found out. This was what worried Nat.

"It's a perfectly bloody mess, darling," he said suddenly, walking back to the bed, "but we must work out something, somehow. Come and watch the dawn break over the mountains—it's glorious. Forget our sorrows. Come and be comforted, and let's enjoy the first sunrise we've ever seen together. *And* pray to all the gods it won't be the last."

3

For Toni the days that followed were the only ones in her life when she was completely satisfied as a woman, totally satisfied with her lover. Familiarity did not breed contempt. She was left with a great respect for Nat. They had a shared sense of humour; they laughed a lot. They agreed to avoid the glitter of crowded Cannes, with the sleek yachts in the harbour; the millionaires running their banks in the Casinos; and the expensive shops on the Croisette.

They stayed higher up—had picnic lunches—explored remote villages, hamlets in the beautiful countryside of the Alpes Maritime; discovered enchanting little cafés and ate well and put on weight. They said they must diet, but didn't.

One day they drove as far as St. Paul de Vence. They fell in love with its exquisite ancient grey stone buildings, the narrow alleys, the archways, the glorious fountain in the Square. All these places and the simplicity and peace and friendliness of their 'togetherness' unfolded a new glorious love of life for Toni.

She refused to go to expensive restaurants. She enjoyed the small places—an omelette; or a plate of fresh fish; the fruits and cheeses of Provence, washed down by a cool *vin-du-pays*.

She lost much of her nervous tension. She was energetic and full of youthful enthusiasm again. To Nat it was quite pathetic to see how much she enjoyed the simple pleasures of life and how grateful she was for his love and all their loving.

Each night they ate dinner at their own hotel, sitting on the terrace. One fat candle in a tall glass wavered its brave light beside a pot of flowers. The sky above was studded with stars. The faint night breeze blew down from the mountains. As darkness fell, fairy lights glowed in the little trees and lit up the huge pink flowers in the hibiscus trees. Their waitress— an olive-skinned dark-eyed girl from the Midi—served the meal—a benevolent smile on her lips, suggesting that she guessed that the handsome Englishman and the *jeune Madame* with the marvellous eyes were on their *lune de miel*.

* * *

At the end of the day, in their own room—now perfumed by a huge bunch of spicy carnations which were so cheap and so profuse in this country—Toni and Nat felt secure, shut away from the world again. Life became all love, all tenderness, all beauty bound up in their profound satisfaction in each other.

Toni said no more about Guy. It was an unspoken agreement that his name should be taboo. But Nat had been right to make her unburden her story, she told herself. She felt strangely peaceful and philosophical now.

Came the evening when it was Nat's turn to talk about himself. It all started when Toni called him "my Nathaniel". Then he smiled and said:

"My mother always called me that. I prefer Nat, myself, *Nathaniel* is a bit much, don't you think?"

"Oh, I like it," said Toni, " but let's just always be Toni and Nat to each other—it's sort of more friendly. Besides—*he* calls me Antonia. So does my aunt. I detest it. Tell me about your mother."

He had loved her deeply, he said. She had inherited both sensibility and artistry from her Jewish father.

He continued at her request to talk about his early life and his gradual rise to success as a gynaecologist. He didn't seem to be particularly close to the man who shared his consulting room—Keith Lucas-Wright. It was purely a business arrangement, but he went occasionally to dine with Keith and his family.

26

"We also share a secretary-receptionist," Nat ended.

"And is she fabulously attractive?" Toni asked with her eyes suddenly full of mischief.

"I wouldn't tell you even if I thought so," he grinned, but quickly went on: "No, poor soul—she's rather pathetic. Not all that young either, thirtyish, perpetually worried about her figure which is on the plump side—a bit of Portuguese blood there, I believe. She has fine dark eyes and wears horn-rims. She seems to have a huge amount of black hair coiled on the top of her head but I wouldn't know if it's hers or a wig—who does know now?"

"I'm relieved," said Toni, still with her tongue in her cheek.

"My *darling* Toni, you need hardly be jealous of poor Miss Withers. She's good with the patients and efficient. That's the only reason we keep her."

"Withers really isn't a glamorous name."

"And it doesn't go with Teresa which is her first name."

"Presumably *Teresa* comes from the Portuguese side."

"As a matter of fact," said Nat with a sudden frown, "I've been wanting to tell you about poor Teresa, and ask your advice. She confided in me the other day, after asking for an advance of her salary, that she has been living for some time with a fellow who works as a film extra. I reckon she's keeping him and that he's pretty useless. But they need money. And she's the real breadwinner."

"Poor, poor Teresa."

"Shall I advise her to get rid of the film extra?"

"No—she wouldn't do it if she loves him. *I* wouldn't get rid of you if I had to work for you and pay all your debts."

"Women are wonderful," said Nat shaking his head, "and what you've just said makes me feel very humble, my darling."

"I love you," said Toni, "and I only hope you won't get tired of me saying so."

"I shall be a worried man if you stop saying so."

Came another day toward the end of their holiday when she persuaded Nat to drive her down to Cannes. When he protested that it might be dangerous, she shrugged—suddenly reckless.

"I doubt it. Cannes is a big town. I know, I've been there several times with Guy. But I do want to go to one special man's shop in the Rue d'Antibes where I'm sure I could find something to give you. Just one little souvenir."

Nat gave in. After all, it was absurd to suppose they might run into a friend during just one single hour in Cannes.

He drove her down the winding hill and into the crazy crush of cars and holidaymakers beside the brilliant blue of the sea. Parking the Triumph was a nightmare but eventually Nat found a place facing the harbour. Arm in arm, he and Toni walked toward the Rue d'Antibes and the shops. Nat suggested a long cold drink in a small restaurant on the Croisette. They wanted to avoid any of the big hotels.

Afterwards, when they discussed what happened that fatal day, they agreed they had made a big mistake. The risk, small though it was, had always been there. There is always the millionth chance that can kill, and their tremendous happiness was murdered with a vengeance on that hot sunlit morning while Nat sat drinking his cold lager and Toni, her iced coffee.

Two fashionably dressed women sauntered towards the open-air café, laughing and talking. In their forties, they were both good-looking, of the hard woman-of-the-world type for whom Nat had little use.

"False eyelashes, false bosoms, God knows what else false," he whispered, as he directed Toni's attention to the newcomers. The women sat down at a table near them, took off their dark glasses and stared around. "A deadly species, to be avoided," added Nat.

Just how deadly he only knew when he saw Toni's golden eyes widen—and her cheeks pale.

"*God!*" she whispered.

"What? You don't *know* them, do you?"

"Yes," she gasped. "It's absolutely *unbelievable*—one of

them is Lady Hollstein, Desmond Hollstein's wife. That one with the blonde hair. Her husband owns an art gallery and is a bosom friend of Guy's. Leila is an absolute bitch and if she recognises me, she'll tell Guy for a certainty."

Nat's face burned suddenly. This was something he had dreaded from the start but had deceived himself into the belief that it would not happen.

"*I know we oughtn't to have come down to this bloody town,*" he whispered.

Worse was to follow.

Toni, with trembling hands, snatched at her dark glasses and put them on. It was too late. The blonde hard-faced woman she called Leila had seen her. Like a cat she pounced, rushed up on her victim.

"*Sweetie...*" The very way she used that endearment made Nat's fingers curl. "Fancy meeting *you* here. Where's Guy? I thought Des said Guy was in Rio pulling off a terrific deal. He's so brilliant, dear Guy."

For a moment Toni really did not know what to reply. She looked desperately at Nat. Leila had reached their table. Nat was standing up—stiff and polite. His lean face was expressionless but Toni knew perfectly well what he was feeling. She stuttered:

"Oh—I—I'm h-here ... with friends."

"Lovely, for you, darling. Anyone I know?"

"I d-don't think so."

Leila Hollstein looked over her shoulder at her friend who was busy rouging her lips.

"You must meet my old friend, Mrs. Thurston. I don't think you two have ever come across each other. She was at school with me. Lives in Jersey. Virginia Thurston. Her husband died a year ago and Gina's been rather seedy since, poor darling. So we both thought we'd totter down here and get some sun and swimming which is good for Gina's muscles."

"Where are you staying?" asked Toni, still seeking

desperately in her mind to find some way out of this *impasse*. Who could she say she was staying with? Whatever lie she told wouldn't prevent Leila, who was a compulsive gossip, from telling all London that she had found Toni in Cannes "*not with her husband, my dear, but with another man.*"

Nat continued to stand there, stiff and dumb, feeling both helpless and furious that this situation had arisen. As was inevitable, Lady Hollstein turned to him and gave him the arch appraising look he received from so many women.

"Aren't you going to introduce me to your friend, Toni?"

"Yes, M-Mr. Gray," Toni continued to stammer, "er-meet —Lady Hollstein."

"Isn't the weather gorgeous, Mr. Gray?" said Leila gaily, still eyeing the tall blue-eyed young man. He looked so brown and well and *so masculine*. She adored tall, lean men and this one had such a *strong* face. Lucky little Toni! Who *was* the boy-friend? Where had she picked him up? Presumably there was a *Mrs*. Gray and Toni must be staying with them, *somewhere*.

Nat agreed with Lady Hollstein that the weather was wonderful—Leila beckoned to her friend. Virginia Thurston rose and joined them. She was red-haired, full-bosomed and lazy-looking but, Nat thought, she had a kinder mouth and was probably less of a cat than her ladyship. She smiled at Toni in a friendly way.

"Delighted to meet you—heard so much about you, Mrs. Brand. Are *you* staying in Cannes, Mr. Gray?"

"No," said Nat quickly and offered no further information. Leila probed, her long artificial lashes flickering at Toni.

"Where have you parked your lovely little self, sweetie?"

Toni felt positively faint all of a sudden and sat down. Of all the women in the world to have run into, Leila Hollstein must be the worst, she thought despairingly. She had never liked her, but Guy was a close friend of Desmond Hollstein and often asked his advice about the purchase or sale of paintings. Toni had always despised Leila's passion for gossip—her total insincerity. Under all that flattery and gushing, she was a spiteful creature. She had married for position and money, had had several boy-friends and kept none of them, and was now frustrated and in search of fresh fields to conquer. Nothing was more dangerous than a frustrated woman when she came across a situation like Toni's. She would begrudge her every little hour of happiness and see that she paid for it. Toni knew.

When Leila repeated her question as to where Toni was staying, Nat deliberately broke in.

"I wish I could offer you both a drink but Toni and I have got to get back to our friends—a lunch party in Cap d'Antibes."

But Leila hung on to this situation with her teeth right in it.

"Oh, are you down here with a party, sweetie?" she asked Toni.

Nat called to a passing waiter.

"*L'addition!*"

Then Toni counter-questioned Lady Hollstein.

"Where are *you* staying?"

"Mougins," answered Leila promptly.

Before Toni and Nat could recover from this mortal blow, Virginia put in a word:

"A divine little hotel. We got there late last night. My only complaint is I've got a small single room and so has Leila, as all the nice doubles are full. We both said we wanted to avoid big hotels and all the noise in Cannes, and as we've got Leila's car and chauffeur, we booked in at this place. It's high up near Grasse and fresher at night. Someone recommended it to us. We haven't seen much of it yet. We came down here directly after our breakfast. We both adore swimming in the sea rather than a *piscine*."

Toni made no comment. She looked at Nat. He returned her gaze but his face was expressionless. He was a man who never lost his head in a crisis. He was still hoping to avert the final catastrophe. There was more than one hotel in Mougins. But he and Toni must nip up to *Mas Candille* immediately, pay the bill and bolt before these two women could get back and ferret them out. The next words Leila Hollstein spoke seemed to him like the *coup de grâce* given by a victorious matador to a dying bull. He mentally felt himself sinking to his knees.

"Our little hotel is called *Mas Candille*," she said brightly. "You must bring your party up to drinks with us and see it, Toni dear."

4

The conversation between Toni and Nat as they drove back to Mougins was terse and distressing to them both. He said:

"We've got to get away before those two women finish their day on the beach."

"We'll be safe if we get away, surely!"

"H'm, you introduced me as Mr. Gray, remember? You had to. Lady Hollstein will talk to Monsieur at *Mas Candille*. He speaks beautiful English and is very friendly. Why shouldn't she find out that a Mr. and Mrs. Gray have been staying there but suddenly and mysteriously had to vacate their room? He could offer it to your friend, couldn't he? She told us that she and the friend hated single rooms."

"Yes, that's so," Toni agreed gloomily.

"And I assure you Monsieur will describe you and the colour of your eyes. Oh, no, my dear, we've had it. The axe has fallen."

"Oh, God, why did I ask you to take me down to Cannes?"

"No use asking 'why' now," he snapped.

His fears for her as well as for himself made him irritable for the first time.

Toni felt suddenly chilled.

"Poor Chris little knew what she was doing when she sent us to Mougins."

"And why the hell had that bitch got to park herself in *Mas Candille*?"

"Because it's famous for charm and good food. Also Leila's friend is convalescing and didn't want a large hotel. Leila

33

will definitely tell Guy and ditch us, Nat."

"Won't Christine swear that you were in Ireland?"

"Yes, but I can't ask her to do any more than she's done."
Nat swore under his breath.

"Hell! I worship the ground you walk on and I'm going
to be the cause of frightful trouble for you. It's murderous."

"Stop a moment. Don't go on driving. I feel sick," said
Toni, and suddenly bent forward, struggling against her
nausea.

They were nearing Val de Mougins, a few miles from their
own village. Nat pulled the car into a grass verge and put an
arm around Toni's shoulders.

"Easy, darling. Keep calm. We'll sort things out. Are you
okay?"

She sat up again, her eyes very large and stricken.

"Yes, I'm okay again. Sorry, I what they call 'came over
queer'."

"Darling, you've had a ghastly shock."

"And it's something we can't laugh off. I suppose we can
tell some story to Monsieur at our hotel about sudden bad
news from home and all that, and we've got enough francs to
pay our bill and move to some other place, but I reckon it's
the end really. We both ought to go home at once."

Nat stayed silent—reflecting. He was a man of precision
and stability. He had at one time prided himself on his
moral strength. This girl, this entrancing woman whose lover
he had become, was the one real weakness of his life—the one
who had found a chink in his armour even though she hadn't
set out to look for it. Now she had become part of his life.
More dear to him than his own honour. And even today
when honour was of less account than it used to be, he had
once prided himself on possessing it. He had once thought
men—especially doctors—who fooled around with other men's
wives—despicable.

Toni had altered all that. Her tragic story, her grim

34

marriage, her complete disillusionment in men, had reached the very core of Nat's being. He had taken her to his heart. She was the only woman to matter to him since his mother died, with the added attraction of intense physical desire. It was no light love that had led Nat to go back on his former scruples and risk his good name by coming away with her. But he certainly wished the holiday had not ended in this way.

"I refuse to let you go back and face this trouble alone," he said suddenly, "that I *won't* do. In fact I shan't let you go back to Guy at all."

She drew away from him, startled.

"For goodness sake, Nat darling, we've agreed—" she began.

He broke in:

"Do you think Lady Hollstein is sure to tell Guy about our meeting?"

"Undoubtedly and he'll cross-question me until I'm sunk. I know him. He'll never let go until he's found out the truth."

Nat hit on a new line of thought:

"I thought he valued you so highly he wouldn't want to lose you. Perhaps he won't *want* to suspect you."

"Yes, he will. In his mind I belong to him. I'm *his*. If he finds out I've spent this week with you and that I am in love with you, he'll be dreadfully vindictive. He'll use all his money and power to ruin us both. I keep telling you that he couldn't really ruin *me* because I'd adore to be divorced for you, but *you'd* suffer. And I won't have that."

"A man can take care of himself."

Toni gave a hollow laugh.

"A doctor can't. Whenever I've read about some medical man being a co-respondent in a divorce case I've always despised the other woman and thought how contemptible she was to risk wrecking his reputation."

"Oh, darling, divorce isn't all that bad these days," Nat tried to comfort her. He was, as always, touched by her solicitude.

35

There followed another argument. He insisted he should come into the open with Guy. Toni obstinately refused to consider it.

She said:

"Maybe if I told Leila the truth and flung myself on her mercy, she'd keep quiet. Mrs. Thurston, too. Anyhow *she* lives in the Channel Islands and doesn't know Guy."

"I won't have you crawling to that Hollstein woman. Anyhow, her type isn't capable of mercy or generosity. She won't consider you."

Despair settled upon Toni again. She knew that Nat was right.

Nat paid the bill. He made a suitable excuse to the sympathetic manager. So now the honeymoon was over. They must set out for Avignon and try to get the car on the next possible train. They agreed that it would be hopeless even to try and finish their holiday in another 'bolt-hole'. They wouldn't enjoy themselves with so much on their minds. Wiser to get back. They also agreed to part in London, sit tight, and await events. For Toni to admit her guilt and appeal to Leila Hollstein would be a mistake. They must wait and see if the news did, in fact, ever reach Guy.

"I don't like it," Nat said, as he shut the last suitcase. "I loathe the idea of you going back to that bastard. It makes me feel a coward and a creep."

"I swear to you, Nat, I'd feel suicidal if I let you take me away and Guy took his revenge on you. And make no mistake, he'll ferret out the fact that Mr. Gray is Mr. Olver."

Nat looked down into her soft tragic eyes.

"You're the most generous, loving girl on earth. I feel a damned weakling letting you go."

"No—you're strong and sensible," she corrected. "And it's been worth it. It's been wonderful. You've shown me heaven. Please, *please*, darling Nat, don't have any regrets."

"I'll never forget one instant of our week here."

"I must powder my nose, then we'd better get off, darling."

For a moment they held on to each other. Then Nat took his cue from Toni. They left *Mas Candille* in grim silence.

* * *

As they drove away Toni did not look back at the charming Provençal inn. The awful sudden departure hurt too much. But she wondered bitterly if Leila Hollstein would indeed be sleeping in *their* room—in *their* bed—tonight.

That next morning after a disturbed night in the *wagon-lit,* they swayed down the passage to the dining car for breakfast. It went to Nat's heart to look at Toni. She was so changed from the radiant girl he had taken to France a week ago.

All too soon they were on the ferry—then on the final lap of their journey, both tired and deeply worried. In England it was cool and drizzling and so very different from the South of France.

The drive down the Dover road to London was little more cheerful. Toni, sunk in troubled thought, was trying to make up her mind how she would act and what she would say if the worst happened at home. Tonight, she decided, she would stay at the penthouse. Tomorrow she would go down to the house in Bray where Mrs. Millin would look after her. Guy would be back on Saturday.

"Nothing will happen at once," she told Nat as they neared London. "After all, Leila's got to come back to town before *anybody* will be told. Oh, Nat, you can't believe how ghastly it will be living with Guy again but it would be much more ghastly if—"

"If I took the rap," he broke in grimly, "yes, I know that's how you feel. But I don't, and I'm fast reaching the pitch when I intend to take it."

She took no notice of this.

"I'll phone you on Monday when I'm back in town. I've

got your flat-number. When will you be in?"

"Between six and seven if you can call me."

"I'll manage it. I know Guy's habits and he rarely alters them. He always has a bath and lies on his bed and reads until he changes—about seven. I'll phone you then, in the call-box down in the main entrance."

"And I'll tell them at the hospital I've cut my holiday short because I thought I was needed," said Nat with some sarcasm. "They'll be only too pleased to see me again."

She stole a look at him. She didn't know much about Nat's private life—only that he shared a flat with his cousin in a large converted house around the corner from Wimpole Street —a stone's throw from his consulting rooms.

His cousin, Mervyn Olver who was a Lieutenant Commander in the Navy, was six years older than Nat—and more often than not at sea—but occupied the flat with Nat when he was on leave. Toni had never met him. Since her involvement with Nat, Mervyn had been in the Far East. He was due home any time now.

Earlier on, Nat had told Toni that he would be glad to see Mervyn again. They shared many tastes. They both enjoyed fishing. They went salmon-fishing in Ireland last spring. Now, if things settled down, he would undoubtedly be glad of his cousin's companionship. Mervyn, once he knew about Toni, would be on Nat's side. He himself had been through one disastrous marriage and several equally disastrous love-affairs. Nat would receive nothing but sympathy and understanding from his cousin. But all that was in the future. The present engrossed Nat—as it did Toni.

He drove her down to the Embankment. He got out of the car and hailed a taxi from the rank. He put Toni's two cases into it and gave the driver a fifty pence piece.

"Take this lady to River Court—"

"It's the entrance to No. 104—the main block," Toni supplemented.

She smiled at Nat but her heart sank to its lowest as she saw her luggage lying there beside the taxi driver. It was awful leaving Nat like this. Almost she broke down and begged him to come with her, or let her go with him to his flat. But she said in a formal voice:

"Thanks awfully for the lift. Goodbye now."

"Goodbye and sorry I couldn't take you all the way," he answered.

But he looked at her and she looked at him through the window as she seated herself in the taxi and they went on looking until she was driven away, and she lost sight of him.

Then she sat motionless clutching her bag, trying to fight her grief and pain.

I wish I were dead, she thought.

But at once she jerked herself back to sanity.

Don't be idiotic, Antonia Brand. Face up to things. This is what you risked and what you knew might happen and all you've got to do now is keep your head—await events and hope for the best. And do stop being so emotional. Stop thinking about Nat, or you'll go round the bend.

5

"You're looking well, Antonia," said Guy Brand pleasantly.

"Thanks, I'm fine," said Toni in a clear bright voice.

She did not want to face her husband as they sat together on the deep-cushioned, chestnut-brown sofa which faced one of the wide windows overlooking the park.

He had only just arrived back from the Airport having telephoned from Rio ordering her to send the Rolls, and Wilson, his chauffeur, to meet him. Delays were expected both ends.

She sat drinking sherry. Guy had just lit a cigar. He rarely smoked anything else. He, too, looked well, Toni thought. He was even plumper than before. There were pouches under the large heavy-lidded eyes, and his neck seemed to have thickened. He was really a big man in all ways, but—she had to admit this—he had distinction.

The reddish gold hair was a little long—touching his collar at the back—but brushed well back from his broad forehead. His near presence, the familiar aroma of his cigar, the knowledge that he was back in her life again with his dominating influence, his watchful eye and latent cruelty, depressed her unutterably. As for that pleasant way in which he remarked on her appearence, she was not deceived into believing that he was in a really amiable mood. He had begun by complaining about the flight, the delays, business associates who had displeased him in some way or other, and the miserable London weather.

"I am surprised to find you so brown after a holiday in

Ireland. You must have had unusual weather," he said.

She moved uneasily. She never knew precisely what lay behind Guy's innocent remarks.

"Oh, it was marvellous over there," she lied unhappily, and changed the conversation, "I've ordered dinner for eight, by the way. I expect you're hungry."

Guy glanced at his wrist-watch.

"Make it half-past. I'm not hungry. Besides I had champagne and smoked salmon on the Boeing."

"I'll ring the restaurant and tell them."

As she moved toward the house-telephone, she felt Guy's plump fingers grab her wrist.

"Don't run away. We haven't seen each other for nearly two weeks. We have a lot to talk about."

She sat down again obediently and reached out to the Limoges box on the small table beside her. She needed a cigarette. Immediately Guy, who was unfailingly courteous, even when he was being his most hateful, snapped on his lighter and held it to her cigarette.

She sat back, inhaling the smoke and looked in a hunted way round the beautiful L-shaped room. It was forty feet long, with an archway leading into a small dining hall. The décor was magnificent; the paintings priceless; the furnishings in perfect taste. Two superb marble and gold stands flanked the tall black marble fireplace. There were vases and bowls with extravagant flower arrangements.

Her white and silver bedroom was just as luxurious. So beautiful that it had taken her breath away when she first saw it after Guy had re-decorated it for his bride. The whole penthouse was fabulous, she thought, beyond the wildest dreams of a girl in her former position. But to her it had never become a home. It was a museum in which she was forced to live. She had no communication with it, any more than she had with Guy himself. It was the same thing in their lovely river home. Where Guy lived there could be neither love nor friendship—only for her, the subjugation of a slave.

She heard his clear precise voice at this moment with the well-known note of disapproval in it:

"You're not paying attention to what I am saying, Antonia."

"Sorry, Guy."

"You always say that. It does irritate me."

"Then I'm *not* sorry," she said with unusual irritation on her part. She had learned that it didn't do to cross swords with her husband. She always got the worst of it.

She saw his eyebrows go up.

"That's rather vulgar—and impertinent and, I must say, unlike you."

"Sorry," she began again and stopped with a giggle. She looked at him with resentful eyes.

"No, I mustn't say that. Oh, *really*, Guy, I never know *what* to say. I'm always in the wrong and I can't open my mouth without you criticising me."

He looked genuinely surprised. He was not accustomed to opposition from his young wife. She was usually docile. At times, he had to confess, it was boring. He would have preferred her to show more fight. Of course he had realised when he had chosen her for his wife that she was a simple sort of child. And he thought he would enjoy turning her into a new and more interesting Antonia. He had imagined her rather more malleable than she had turned out to be. In the beginning it had been better. She had fought back hotly when he said or did things she disliked, especially during their more intimate moments. Lately she had become lethargic.

Looking at her this evening he had to admit he had never seen her look more attractive. Was it his imagination or had her hollowed cheeks filled out? He had told her not so long ago that she was growing too thin and should eat more. He had sent her to a specialist about her nerves, too, and been annoyed when the neuro-physician informed him that there was absolutely nothing wrong with Mrs. Brand except that she needed more rest and was leading too hectic a life, with too many social engagements. And that she should have more opportunity to relax.

Guy had detected a note of personal reproach about this diagnosis. But he lied to Antonia and told her the man had said there was nothing wrong with her, that she imagined her ills, and accused her of deliberately starving herself in order to keep her slender line, and had allowed her nerves to get the better of her.

Now he took his cigar from his mouth with his right hand and laid his left one on her knee. She had already changed into a fashionable short housecoat—dark blue and silver Persian silk with a high collar and a choker of sapphires—the beautiful jewels he had given her for Christmas. Her new surprising tan suited her, he decided.

"I don't wish to criticise or upset you, my dear," he said easily. "Tell me more about your holiday with your friends. Personally of course I find both Christine and Joseph deadly dull, I don't know why you like them."

Toni's head shot up.

"They're sweet people and Chris is my greatest friend."

"Well, as long as I don't have to be bored by them, you can go on seeing them," said Guy, his small lips puckered into a tight little smile.

She hated him. She hated everything he said or did and she loathed the feeling of his hot, possessive hand against her silk-clad thigh. She tried wildly to keep her composure and not to push that hand away and scream her hatred of him aloud. She kept having to tell herself that she deserved whatever was coming because she had chosen to break her marriage vows. Hundreds of women did so without scruple but she was not as hard or permissive in her outlook as some of them. In addition Toni had to keep reminding herself fiercely that she must not say the wrong thing and give Nat away.

So she submitted to that detested hand that patted and

stroked her as though she were a cat. She tried to answer Guy's questions lightly and with conviction.

She had already been primed by Chris about the Irish hotel and the beauties of Connemara. She managed to lie—on and on—because Guy went on and on with his probing. How big was the hotel? What sort of room did she have? How had she spent her days? What was the food like? Toni made only one glaring slip—at least to her, it seemed to glare.

"Tell me about the air ferry? Would it be worth my while to fly the Rolls over? I might take you there for a week-end. I've never seen Ireland. Not been particularly interested. But you make it sound fascinating."

Then she stumbled. She had forgotten to ask Chris's husband about the ferry. And she couldn't remember anything about the Airport. She just blurted out the word "Shannon" hoping for the best. Guy never took his stony grey gaze from her and she could feel her cheeks burning. They burned redder when he added:

"If that hotel you stayed in was so comfortable we'll book there. I believe Connemara is one of the most beautiful lakes in the world. I'll use that new camera of mine with the wide-angled lens. I'll tell my secretary to book a room before the summer completely ends. I'll mention your name as, of course, the manager will remember you. Who forgets Mrs. Guy Brand?" he added smoothly.

The sweat broke out on Toni's forehead.

That's done it, she thought. *He's suspicious. He doesn't quite know why, but he is. I am idiotically nervous and I loathe telling barefaced lies—I know I've boobed somewhere. He's beginning to wonder whether I went to Ireland at all. He's so terribly perceptive—my God!*

Guy removed his hand and let the fine ash fall from his cigar into an ashtray. His puckered little mouth was smiling.

"Well, well," he continued. "How intriguing about your splendid holiday. I must make a point of asking Joseph for a drink at the Club. He can tell me more about Ireland and taking the car over."

Guy never uses nicknames. 'Joe' must be Joseph. Just as she was Antonia. He was very punctilious and pompous.

She put a hand up, and with the wisp of chiffon which she called a handkerchief, dabbed her brow. This really *was* getting dangerous. Chris could be relied upon. She was cool, and if not good at deception, she would never let her friend down. But Joe was different. He was a very nice creature—one of the best—but more simple. (Men are often so much more simple than women some of whom seem to thrive on intrigue.) Guy, with his glib tongue and outward show of good humour, would soon have poor honest Joe in knots and learn that she hadn't been in Ireland with them at all. Whatever happened, she must telephone Chris tomorrow and tell her to warn Joe not to accept any invitation from Guy.

"I'm surprised you find it so warm in here, my dear," said Guy, "your little face looks quite damp."

She could no longer endure this inquisition. It was playing havoc with her nerves. She resorted to a crazy show of false gaiety and sprang to her feet.

"It's nice to have you home. I'll put on one of your favourite records. What would you like? That delicious little piece of Mozart you bought just before you went to Rio? I know I am not as keen on the classics as you are but I thought that one so gay and beautiful—and he was very young when he wrote it, wasn't he? I must get more Mozart's records and—"

"For heaven's sake, Antonia," Guy broke in, his voice no longer agreeable. "I don't want Mozart at this moment and what on *earth's* the matter with you? Why don't you sit down and keep calm and tell me more about your holiday? Or weren't you a good girl in Ireland?" He suddenly shot the words—still smiling. "Is there something I ought to know? I've never seen you in such a state. You're quite hysterical. And *don't* tell me you're really glad to see me, I can't believe it."

She stood still, her heart pounding—her eyes looking at him with the expression of a trapped creature.

"I don't understand you, you're so *peculiar!*" she said. "But you always are. I can never feel *myself* with you. You make me hysterical."

He laid down the stump of his cigar, came up to her and gripped her arms so tightly that they hurt. Under their heavy lids his eyes seemed to her like gimlets boring into her. She was so confused she didn't know what to say—how to act. In this hour she almost felt that the glorious days and nights at Mougins had not been worth while. The cost was too heavy. If only she dared leave this monster who thought himself so civilised, and go to Nat. But she must stand alone.

"Well?" Guy said. "*Is* there something I ought to know?"

Then she pulled herself together.

"No, there isn't," she said through her teeth. "You try to fight with me as soon as you get home. Why? Why don't you leave me alone? You're a big bully!"

An instant's silence. Tears started to gush from Toni's eyes and pelt down her cheeks. The sight of them, added to what she had just said, seemed suddenly to appeal to Guy's warped sense of humour. He let her go, threw back his head and gave one of his rich throaty chuckles.

"Well, *well*. I *have* upset my poor little wife! And her eyes are so magnificent—like gorgeous jewels when they are diamonded by tears. However stupid and irritating you may be, my pet, I never fail to be stirred by your fantastic beauty. You must retain your new glowing tan. It's most effective. Now stop being so silly and I'll go and dress, then we'll have a nice friendly meal. Afterwards, perhaps, we'll go along to Annabel's and dance. I've been sitting in that damn plane for about eight hours and I'd rather like some exercise. We haven't danced for a long time, have we, pet?"

Waving a plump white hand gracefully in her direction, he walked out of the room.

She sank back on the sofa and covered her face with her

hands. There was nothing she wanted to do less than go out and dance with Guy. She was far too tired and worried.

She went to her own room and swallowed a couple of pain-killing tablets. Then she brushed the silky hair that Nat, *dear* Nat, had kissed and played with and adored.

I've just got to go through with this, she told herself.

She tried hard to be friendly and talk normally with Guy while they ate the expensive meal sent up by one of the excellent chefs in the River Court restaurant. Iced Vichysoisse, tournadoes with *maître d'hôtel* butter and the special lemon-ice that Guy liked, followed by Stilton cheese and port. He kept asking her to eat more. But Toni felt she would be sick if she swallowed another mouthful.

*   *   *

He seemed in a better mood when they set out, just before ten, for Annabel's Night Club. She would have given anything to be allowed to go to bed and sleep. He talked to her as only Guy could talk—full of interesting anecdotes about his recent work and social activities in South America. But Toni wasn't impressed, least of all when he mentioned that he wished to take her to Rio next year. She sat in the Rolls, a small figure huddled in the short sable jacket she had put on because it was so unseasonably cold this September night. If anything served to lighten her darkness it was the belief that Guy was not really suspicious about Ireland; that she had imagined it. She had been unnecessarily alarmed. He was being really friendly now.

He remained in a good mood—dancing with her quite often, complimenting her, pleased when they met an important friend who paid her a fulsome compliment.

"I must say I'm always very proud of my attractive wife," Guy observed.

Yes, she thought bitterly, *just as you are of your Renoir or Graham Sutherland or Picasso or any of your other valuable possessions.*

47

Her headache returned in full force just before midnight. She asked Guy to take her home. He did so, to her surprise, without opposition. But she was considerably startled and roused from that feeling of deadly weariness once they were back in the penthouse. For he said, smiling:

"Have a good night's rest, my dear. You won't have to put up with me. I've moved my things into my dressing room."

Her large eyes stared at him. Once or twice when she had suggested she might like to sleep alone he had categorically refused.

Normally, she would have been deeply thankful to have her bed to herself—be free to weep into her pillow if she wanted to, and to think about Nat.

But now it was her turn to be suspicious.

Why should Guy have decided not to sleep with her tonight? With what object in view? *Unless he really did suspect infidelity and was not going to place himself in a position— should the possibility of divorce arise—of having condoned it?*

6

For a further week Toni wondered how she was going to carry on without cracking up completely.

Guy's strange attitude—that move, for instance, from her bedroom to his own—his continued pleasantness, both baffled and unnerved her.

Her only contact with Nat had been two brief telephone calls after he got home. On neither occasion had she worried him by mentioning her fears that Guy suspected her. He had no special news for her.

As far as they both knew, Leila had not yet seen or spoken to Guy.

Out of sheer curiosity, Toni had phoned the Hollsteins during this week but been told that "her laydship was still away".

Guy now put Toni through a gruelling time. She had to cope with a crowded social programme. Four nights running they entertained guests who were business contacts of Guy's. He even insisted she should lunch with him daily—something he had never done before. His constant attentions exhausted her. Once he playfully suggested that he was growing jealous. "Like a devoted lover," he said smiling, and watched her discomfiture and that traitorous colour rise to her cheeks.

*   *   *

They were at Bray for the following weekend. The housekeeper was on holiday, so Toni pleaded to be allowed to rest from social activities until the Monday—to which Guy agreed. So he asked no friends down to stay. They were alone.

Toni found this almost worse. On Saturday morning before lunch, she stayed in bed till late, then came down and settled herself on the sofa. She still felt utterly depleted and depressed. A log-fire was burning in the handsome grate. The September day was cool and wet.

Toni wondered how in God's name she could slip out, unseen by Guy, and telephone Nat today. After the past week of separation and silence she felt desperate. She could not go on being practical or brave. She even wondered miserably if Nat had forgotten her. He led such a busy life.

Guy suddenly walked into the room with a letter in his hand. Toni looked up at him, noting the mean little smile on his lips. She prepared herself for something disagreeable. He had already told her on a previous occasion that he was annoyed because he had invited Christine's husband for a drink, and been refused. But she did not dream until now that he had written to the holiday hotel in Connemara.

He tossed an envelope with the Irish stamp on to Toni's lap.

"Do read this, my dear."

Her heart thumped. She read the letter:

"Dear Sir,
In answer to your esteemed letter concerning a booking here, I shall be pleased to let you have the sort of suite you require next summer but we close down at the end of next week. I also regret that I cannot find any trace of a Mrs. Guy Brand having stayed here on the date you mention. I think you must have written to the wrong hotel. . ."

Toni clenched her fingers. She neither looked up at her husband nor moved. She felt petrified. But she must try to keep Nat out of this at all costs.

"Well? What do you say to that?" Guy asked, taking back the envelope.

"Nothing."

He looked down at Toni, noting her extreme pallor and her expression.

"Come along, Antonia. You can't say *nothing*—like that."

"But I do. Or if you like to put it the other way, I *won't* say anything. You just don't believe I spent my holiday in Ireland."

"Exactly." He shot the word at her viciously.

"Well, Chris will tell you that I did."

"But I won't take Christine's word for it. Also I now understand why your friend Joseph refused to meet me at the Club. *He* knows, and men don't like being involved in these matters. And I dare say, if the truth be known, he isn't all that keen on supporting your alibi. Men generally stand by each other. I'm sure he wouldn't like *his* wife to make a cuckold of her husband."

She adopted a more casual tone and even managed a laugh.

"Really, Guy, you're being ridiculous. What *do* you mean... *cuckold?* The hotel has made a mistake or maybe they keep no records. I signed no book and Chris arranged the room."

"I can easily fly over to Ireland tonight and find out."

Toni sat up, cheeks flaming.

"Even if I admit that I was *not* actually in the same hotel as Chris and Joe—it doesn't prove a thing. I sent you a letter from Connemara—Mrs. Millen had a card too. Didn't you get yours?"

"Oh, yes," he drawled. "Too easy. Alibis—cover-ups—clues to this and to that—quite like a bit of film-fiction. You've been looking too much at T.V., my dear."

Her throat felt dry. She wished passionately that she need not go on lying. She hated it. Her dizzy brain hit on a desperate little plan.

"Very well, Guy, I'll confess—I actually got as far as the hotel, in Connemara, then decided I couldn't face it. It looked so uncomfortable. So I sent off my mail and decided to take a holiday by myself. I came back to England. I—I just wandered around—that's all."

He pouted at her and shook his head.

"Poor little Antonia. Nothing you say holds water. I've never listened to such a pack of ridiculous muddled lies."

In a panic, Toni flung herself back on the cushions, twisting her long nervous fingers spasmodically together. She supposed she had been idiotically naïve.

"Hadn't you better tell me the truth now?" Guy spoke again.

"No."

"My dear—surely you didn't just spend your holiday whirling in space?"

"No."

"You looked so well when I first came home," he went on, "I noted that tan. Where did you get it? Not down here. And don't say 'Yes' because I can easily ask Mrs. Millen and even if she backs you up, I'll ferret the truth out of one of our dailies. The tradespeople also will know this place was empty while I was away there was no special food ordered except for Mrs. Millin."

Toni looked at him with hatred.

"Do as you like. Ask everybody. I am not going to tell you where I went, or why I didn't stay in Ireland."

Now he frowned. This was a harder Toni than he could usually bully.

"Look, Antonia, are you just being stubborn? You must know you can't get away with these idiotic stories."

"Oh, leave me alone! Stop cross-questioning me. You can twist every word I say. You're so clever. I'm not. And if I say I just wanted to get away from everything and everybody and not tell you or *anyone* where I went, you wouldn't believe me."

He laughed.

"Quite so. Besides—you don't like being alone, Antonia. I know you too well. Who was your companion?"

His cold cruel eyes terrified her. She thought:

I'm not doing too well for you, Nat. Oh, God, if I could only end all this and tell the truth. If only you just weren't a surgeon—weren't so well known—oh God, God, God. What a ghastly mess! Guy wouldn't even make it a quiet divorce. He'd tear your reputation apart.

Guy interrupted her distracted thoughts.

"You've got a secret lover, haven't you, Antonia?" he asked softly. *"Who is he?"* He gripped her wrist suddenly.

Her heart gave a fierce jerk.

"Let go of me, Guy."

"Not until you've told me the name of the man."

"I don't admit there is—a man," she forced the lie.

"You will by the time I've finished with you."

"I won't. You've no right to try and force me to say there is a—a man. Anyhow you lead a life of your own. I am entitled to mine." She broke off with an hysterical sob.

"Oh no, you're not. My wife is *my* wife."

"You're like a savage slave-trader."

"Being rude will get you nowhere."

"Well, I won't stay here to be tormented by you. If you don't stop, Guy, I shall leave you."

For a moment there was silence. Suddenly Guy broke into one of his sinister chuckling laughs.

"Well, well," he said, "at least you've managed to be brave today. It's quite amusing. So the outraged little Antonia threatens to leave me. *Who for?"*

"Nobody," was her desperate answer.

"Back to life with Aunt Penny," he suggested, laughing again. "My *dear,* I thought I'd raised your standards of living and taught you to enjoy being the wife of a millionaire."

"Well, you haven't. You're so cruel and horrible. I can't stand living with you any more. I won't live with Aunt Penny either. I'll go away by myself."

She tried to wrench her wrist away from Guy's fingers. He admired her slim graceful body. She was wearing dark blue slacks with a white cashmere pullover. She looked very young and desirable. But what he felt was no normal desire. And he was obsessed with the wish to dominate her mind.

"Antonia," he said, "you can't get away with this."

"And if I want to leave you, you can't keep me against my will!"

This brought another laugh from Guy. But he kept hold of her wrist.

"Leave me, dear Antonia, but within a few hours I'll have you followed and found. I shall engage the best private investigator in London. I shall also find out who you go to. You'll have to contact *him* once you've left me, won't you?"

She felt frozen with fear for Nat again.

"I refuse to admit that I have a lover," she said, licking her dry lips. "And if you carry on like this, I won't just run away, I'll kill myself. I swear it. . . . *I'll kill myself.*"

Silence. One of the logs fell out of the grate and started to smoke in the fireplace. Guy let go of Toni, stooped, picked the log up with a pair of wrought-iron pinchers, and put it back with the others where it sparked and burst into flames.

He said nothing. He was a cautious man and he began to think coolly about the situation. From what he knew of his young wife, he found it in fact hard to believe that she was capable of taking a lover—daring to deceive him. He knew she was frightened of him. But after listening to her hysterical explanation, he was sure she had done *something* wrong.

He felt no guilt himself. He was a self-satisfied, arrogant man and in his own estimation, never wrong. He considered he had honoured Toni by marrying her.

However, her threat to commit suicide might not be an idle one. He wanted to punish her if he could prove her guilty but not drive her to her death. He was like a large cat playing with a frightened mouse and he did not intend to be deprived of the pleasure. Added to which, her suicide would react unfavourably on him. He would not even be able to maintain in a Coroner's Court that she had always been unstable. Her own doctor would testify that it was he—Guy—who was entirely responsible for her nervous state.

He decided to take another course of action.

He looked at Toni huddled there on the sofa, hunted and miserable. He half pitied her. He had her so completely in his power.

"Come, come—let's talk more sensibly, my dear child."

"Child!" She echoed the word bitterly. "Nobody married to you could remain a *child*."

"Now, please, don't let's argue any more," he said affably. "I know now definitely that you were not in Ireland with your friends. Very well. You had a change of heart and decided to holiday somewhere else. We might any of us do just that. You are silly not to tell where you did, in fact, go. But if you feel you must make a mystery of it, I'll try to put the best construction on things. You're a silly stubborn little girl. But I do not want you to leave me."

Her wonderful eyes stared in amazement. This sudden change of tune did little to make her less nervous, but she tried rather vainly to believe that there might after all be a tolerant, more human side to Guy. She felt this still more when he suddenly picked up her right hand, kissed it and said:

"Do you hate me so much that you'd want to kill yourself, Antonia? I can't tell you how badly that thought shocks me."

She went on staring at him stupidly. She could hardly believe her own hearing.

"I promise I'll accept your explanation—feeble though it is. I was angry and suspicious at first but knowing you I'm sure you did nothing wrong."

She bowed her head. She felt hypocritical and wretched.

"What can I do to make you feel better?" asked this new kindly Guy.

She stood up—shivering.

"Just leave me alone. I don't feel well."

"Poor little Antonia—go back to bed. Have a real rest. Come down and lunch with me later on. And let's have a pleasant evening. I'll play you some records—nothing too heavy—something *you* shall choose."

For the rest of that day she felt terrified even though Guy kept his word and left her alone. But she could not trust him. No one could ever get away with anything with *Guy*.

Before lunch she saw from her window that he was out in the garden. She lifted the phone and dialled the number of Nat's flat—a thing she had never done before during a weekend. She was hardly surprised to get no reply. It left her more than ever depressed.

* * *

When they returned to town after the weekend, she still felt off-colour and tense, although Guy continued to be pleasant.

Toward the middle of that week she began to feel so disturbed, she was driven to contact Nat again.

She called his flat just before dinner, using the phone-box in the entrance hall.

Once she heard his voice say "*Hullo,*" she breathed a sigh of relief.

"Oh, Nat, *Nat!*" she cried.

"Darling, how wonderful to hear you. Are you alone? Can we speak?"

"Yes."

"I've been wondering how the hell you've been getting on but I didn't dare ring you."

"Same with me. I didn't dare either. Besides we've been down in Bray."

"Is everything all right? Have you heard whether that damn woman is back from Cannes?"

"I tried to find out this morning and they said she was still abroad but expected back some time this week."

"We might have been tormenting ourselves unnecessarily. She may never spill the story."

"No, she may not but—"

"What, darling?"

An instant's silence. Toni needed all her strength of mind not to tell Nat about Guy and the letter from Ireland. *She mustn't.* Guy was still being so kind and surprisingly considerate. She must not upset and worry Nat unnecessarily.

"Are you there, my love?" came Nat's voice. That charming and reassuring voice that always made her feel better.

"Yes, my darling."

"Nothing wrong?"

"N—no," Toni stammered and laughed. "Everything's okay and Guy is being very nice at the moment. He's even letting me have my bedroom to myself."

"I couldn't be more relieved."

Toni closed her eyes.

"What have *you* been doing?"

"Up to the eyes in work, darling. Had several rather tricky private cases. I expect you've read about Princess Catrine of Montracine. You remember she had great difficulty in producing the original son and heir? Yes—well, this time twins were indicated and a tricky condition was feared. They asked if I'd fly over for the birth."

"How marvellous. Did you enjoy Montracine?"

"I did. I thought the Princess a charming and very brave girl and *he*—the Prince—delightful. All went well with the twins, thank goodness. I scarcely had time to tour the island, although from what I did see, I'd say it is just the sort of lovely lonely place for us."

"We'll go there one day," Toni said wanly.

"The Prince has actually invited us. He said I was to bring my wife, if I was married, and stay at the Palace one weekend."

Again silence from Toni. There was an empty sickening feeling in her heart. She would never be Nat's wife, she thought. Never go with him to the enchanted Island of Montracine.

"Toni—sweetheart—are you still there?"

"Yes," she said in a hard bright voice and was glad he could not see the tears that were beginning to roll down her cheeks.

"I've had a letter from Cousin Mervyn. He looks forward to joining me. Wants me to fix him up with some shooting this autumn."

"Super," said Toni mechanically.

But she was thinking: *His life is not mine. What he arranges is not for me. Soon our week together in Mougins will seem like a dream—something that never happened. I'll lose him and I'll have to accept it because I have no right to try and keep him or ever risk his good name again. I can even hope my threat to leave Guy or kill myself has startled him into behaving in a more bearable fashion.*

Nat, unaware of her wretched state of mind, told her there'd been some difficulty at the hospital lately—a need to raise money for new equipment. Also, he said, his partner, Keith Lucas-Wright, was growing more of a bore every day. Nat had dined with him at his house in Richmond Park last night. A lot of "stuffed shirts" there—the sort of ultra-conventional type of medical man with that restricted attitude toward life that he couldn't stand.

"As for Keith's own wife, Norma—" Nat continued, "you know I told you about her before—she's one of these awful snobs and name-droppers—and hardly opens her mouth without claiming that she knows dukes and duchesses. Of course she secretly hopes her darling Keith will get a title one day."

Toni was in far too miserable a state of mind to enjoy his humour, but did her best, then added:

"Norma is attractive, isn't she?"

"Good-looking, yes; rather nice figure for the mother of two; red hair—quite striking. But oh, God, Toni, there isn't a woman that can blot out the memory of your lovely little face."

The tears went on rolling down Toni's cheeks.

"Nothing blots out your face for me, either. When is cousin Mervyn arriving?"

"Quite soon. You must meet him. I *must* let him get to know you. He'll be as safe as a house about us. He's my greatest friend as well as my cousin."

"I wonder whether we'll ever be able to meet in the future," Toni blurted out despairingly.

"Darling, that sounds drastic. Are you really all right?"

"Yes ... but I must go now. Guy will look for me."

"Hell," said Nat, "Goodbye, best beloved. Phone me soon again."

"Do you still love me?" She asked the woman's age-old question on a note of despair.

The affirmative came, unhesitating and strong. She put down the receiver.

She went up to the penthouse just in time to see Guy come out of his bedroom—*only just in time*. Her torture began again, her fear of the future, her guilt because of the past, her mistrust of Guy's new amiability.

He suggested drinks. He seemed in good humour. *Seemed,* she thought.

All went well until their evening meal had been served and cleared away. Guy wanted to stay home this evening because he had an early start next morning. He was taking the Rolls up to the Midlands on business. While he was lighting his cigar and talking about his latest project, the telephone rang.

"I'll answer it," said Guy.

Toni was disinterested. She sat on the sofa looking with detached gaze at the emerald ring on her right hand. Her "*status quo*", she thought ironically. Guy was annoyed when she failed to wear the emerald, just as though the fact that the fabulous jewel for which he had paid thousands of pounds bound her to him irrevocably. She heard his voice:

"Oh, *hullo*, Leila. How are you? And how's Desmond? Is he still in Paris organising that Exhibition?"

Silence.

All the colour left Toni's cheeks. Her heart commenced to beat violently and rapidly. She clenched her fingers so tightly together that the sharp diamonds framing the big emerald bit into her flesh. It was a moment of terror that she would never forget.

And she didn't know what Leila Hollstein was saying to Guy.

7

It seemed to Toni that Guy was having a surprisingly lengthy telephone conversation with Leila Hollstein. Usually he ignored her. This evening he was deeply interested in what she was saying. When it was his turn to speak, it was in a low voice; the phone was at the other end of the long salon, and Toni could only catch odd words such as: *"Oh, really,"* *"How very interesting!"* *"Who did you say?"* ... and finally ... *"No, I can't say I've met him, but Toni has so many friends who bore me. I don't waste time on them."*

Toni's throat felt dry. At last she heard him say:

"Hold the line and I'll ask her to have a word with you. Give my regards to Desmond."

Guy then came forward with a pleasant smile.

"Leila wishes to speak to you, my dear."

She was not misled by that smile. By now she was absolutely sure her worst fears were about to be realised. In a curious way she did not feel as panic-stricken as was usual in an hour of disaster. She braced herself to meet it. She said quite lightly:

"Tell her I've just gone to bed, will you, and I'll ring her tomorrow."

Guy bade Leila goodbye, then walked toward the brown satin sofa on which Toni was sitting. He eyed her carefully. She was smoking. She was looking particularly attractive this evening, he thought, although she'd put on too much colour in the attempt to conceal the paleness of her face. But she gave him a timid smile that would have broken the heart of any man but Guy Brand.

"Well, how's our Leila?" she asked brightly.

He sat down beside her and took off his horn-rim glasses. He now gave her the full stare of his grey sphinx-like eyes. They mesmerised her. She had to stare back.

"Well? How was she?" Toni repeated.

Then he bent over her, dug his fingers into her shoulder-blades and brought that detested face of his close to hers.

"You damned little liar!"

Toni's tongue seemed to cleave to the roof of her mouth. She told herself that if she didn't keep calm, she would be lost. More important to her than that, *Nat* would be lost.

"Who is Mr. Gray?" Guy asked. He was breathing hard, noisily.

"Mr. Gray?" Now Toni repeated the name with a nervous giggle. "Oh, yes—how stupid of me! You know how vague I am. I completely forgot he was with me when I met Leila and that friend of hers down in Cannes. Yes, I went to Cannes. Now you know my secret."

She gabbled on crazily, playing for time. For some miracle to happen that would make Guy believe every word she said and take that awful malicious look off his face. "I did go to France. I had a sudden longing for sun and warmth and to be alone, so I flew down to Nice. I didn't stay at any one place. I—" She broke off, for Guy with a swift spiteful movement had thrown her back against the cushions. There was no smile on his face. No pleasantness in his voice now.

"What a rotten liar you are," he said. "Incredibly naïve."

She felt unable to breathe—but went on with her hopeless effort to climb out of the ghastly morass in which she found herself. A morass of lies, deceit, intrigue, all the things that were fundamentally repugnant to her. Other lovers got away with a stolen week, but she and Nat—no! They had been unlucky as well as over-optimistic.

She could see that Guy was furiously angry.

"Tell me who Mr. Gray is and where you met him, because if you don't, I shall keep you here on that sofa all night if need be, and go on asking you questions until you decide to speak."

Contrary to his expectations, Toni stood up and defied him.

"All you need is to shine bright lights in my eyes for Nazi interrogation and torture," she said with sarcasm.

He caught hold of her arm and twisted it.

"*Who is this Mr. Gray?* That's what I want to know and what I intend to find out. Tell me the truth this time."

She gasped:

"Let go. You'll break my arm. If you stop bullying me and talk to me decently I—I'll tell you."

"Very well. You say you went to the South of France *and* wandered around. How did you meet Mr. Gray and who is he?"

"I met him on the Comet going over to Nice. We sat next to each other—and talked. He said that if I were in Cannes he would like to—to meet me and give me a drink. So we—we met for coffee in a bar on the Croisette, that morning Leila saw us."

"And that was the one and only time you contacted him?"

"Yes, of course."

But she saw the sneering disbelief in Guy's eyes, and thought:

Nat, Nat, I'm no good at this sort of thing. Nat, what shall I say next?

"I presume he fell for you?"

"Yes, he did," she said recklessly. "And lots of women fall for *you.*"

"I never lie to you, nor am I unfaithful, Antonia," he said in his iciest voice.

No, she thought, *you're incapable of decent, honest sex.*

"What was Mr. Gray doing in Cannes?" Guy continued, "Was he staying in the same hotel as you?"

"No," she lied frantically.

"And where *were* you staying the night before you ran into Leila?"

Toni was trapped and she knew it. Whatever she answered would be useless—she knew that, too. Guy could and would if necessary ferret out the facts through an Investigation Bureau —no matter what it cost him. Even if it meant combing Cannes or the hotels in the immediate vicinity, to trace her movements—through Air ticket bureaux—Passport office— any of them could furnish him with vital clues. He would try it all, in her name as well as *Mr. Gray's*. Then Guy delivered his final blow.

"I know more than you think, you little fool."

Toni went to pieces.

"I can't stand any more. Let me go. *Let me go!*"

"Not until you've told me the truth. Mr. Gray is your secret lover, isn't he? And you must have known him before you met on the aircraft and arranged it all. You've never been the sort of girl to indulge in sudden promiscuous nights of love. *You knew this man,* didn't you? Tell me. If you don't, I'll soon find out. I'll go to Mougins and take your photograph with me and find out who this man is and if you stayed with him. I'll make him pay until neither of you will feel your so-called honeymoon was worth while."

Toni broke out passionately:

"I won't admit anything. Whatever I've done, it's not as bad as the things you've done to *me*. Things I can't prove because you've got one face for the world and another for me. You don't deserve love and loyalty, and if you think that *this* . . ." she twisted the emerald ring off her finger and threw it at him . . . "is the sort of thing that makes life worth while for me, you're wrong. You're a terrible man and I wish I had died before I ever married you."

For a moment Guy was so surprised by this onslaught, he kept silent. Then he said:

"Leila told me a fascinating story about your Mr. Gray. She and her friend stayed at a little hotel called *La Mas Candille*. I know it quite well. Charming place, isn't is?"

Toni made no reply.

Guy went on, smiling:

"Leila said the manager there is a delightful chap. He mentioned in course of conversation that the only other English people there this month were a Mr. and Mrs. Gray. He actually described them, and Leila said she was sure he, anyhow, was *your* Mr. Gray."

Still no word from Toni. The last drop of colour drained from her cheeks. The rouge stood out in an ugly way on her cheek-bones, and robbed her face of all its charm. But Guy was enjoying himself.

"Leila also said Monsieur thought Madame Gray one of the most beautiful girls he had ever seen, and that she had most unusual eyes—topaz-yellow, he described them. Poetic man, obviously. You have topaz eyes, haven't you, my sweet?"

Toni shut those tell-tale eyes, wishing to God that she had never been born with them; wishing indeed that she had never been born at all.

Leila had done her worst. Bitch. *Bitch!* Toni thought in a sudden passion of resentment. She had guessed the truth and wasn't going to let Toni get away with it. She was a jealous malicious woman and—not unlike Guy—derived acute satisfaction from inflicting pain on others.

Guy snarled at Toni:

"*You* were the Mrs. Gray with topaz eyes staying in that hotel. There's little doubt about it. Leila didn't actually say so but remarked on the odd resemblance this Mrs. Gray bore to you, and the even more odd fact that no other girl looking like you was staying in the hotel. At a moment's notice, Monsieur told her you paid your bill, and were out of the hotel before Leila and her friend got back. Unfortunate isn't it, that your hideout was discovered and your little plan went so wrong."

Before he could speak again, Toni rushed out of the room and slammed the door behind her. She was in a state of complete hysteria now. Only one thing was clear—*Guy knew*—and he would find out a lot more once he set to work. She could not face this thing alone any longer. She must go to Nat—whatever the consequences.

She was so afraid that Guy might lock her in the flat and keep her there, she ran—just as she was—out into the corridor. Then she was in the lift and down in the main entrance, before Guy had time to follow.

* * *

She knew she must cut an odd figure in front of the headporter who was still on duty. Because it was a cool night she had put on an *après-ski* suit, bell-bottom slacks of grey wool; a tunic with a high silver embroidered collar and long chiffon sleeves. She had not had time to snatch a coat. She ran past the astonished porter, and out of the building. At that moment a taxi drew up. Her one piece of good fortune, she thought. A man got out and paid the fare. She took his place and gave the address of Nat's flat.

"It's just off Wimpole Street," she said breathlessly.

Once in the taxi, she huddled in a corner, her face hidden in her hands. She tried to calm down. She began to realise what she had done. She had run away from Guy without luggage—without even a bag. She was penniless.

But of course, if Nat was at home he'd soon pay the fare. He would look after her. He would *have* to, now. She was so scared of Guy she could never possibly go back to him.

I've burned my boats, she thought.

Despair settled over her like a black cloud. She wondered if luck would be on her side and if she would find him in his flat.

* * *

When the taxi stopped outside the tall Georgian house where Nat occupied the first floor, she realised that if Nat were *not* in, she could not pay her taxi.

She stepped out into a drizzle of rain which didn't make things any better, told the driver to wait and ran to the front door. There were only three flats in this converted house.

She examined Nat's card over one of the three bells. *Mr. Nathaniel Olver.* She pressed his bell again and again. Nobody answered and she could see no lights in the first-floor, balconied windows. Her heart sank.

The taxi driver called to her.

"Not allowed to park here, Miss."

"Just wait a moment," she called back, then walked down the steps into the basement and knocked on the porter's door. An elderly man wearing spectacles opened the door. He held an evening paper in one hand and a pipe in the other.

"Yes, Miss, what can I do for you?"

"I've come to—to see Mr. Olver."

"Oh, Mr. Olver—yes. Don't 'e answer 'is bell?"

"No."

"Then he must be out."

"Yes," said Toni patiently, "he's out. I suppose you don't know when he'll be back?"

"Sorry, Miss, I don't."

"It's like this—" Toni delved into the recess of her battered mind, "I—I expected to find him in. He told me he would be. I—I'm his sister. Could you let me into the flat? I know he would want you to."

"Oh, you're his sister," said the porter and blinked at her over his glasses. He saw no reason to disbelieve this pretty young lady. He liked and respected Mr. Olver. The Doctor, he called him. He hadn't half been good to his wife when she had a bad turn. Didn't charge them a shilling. They had no time to send for their National Health man.

"Of course I'll let you in, Miss, and I'm sure Mr. Olver will be back any moment. Miss Olver, is it?"

"Yes."

Lies—lies—always lies, Toni thought wretchedly. Necessity to tell them built up. One seemed to pass from one deception

67

to another, but what did it matter if the porter believed that she was Nat's sister?

The man fetched his duplicate key. As he came back, having put on his uniform jacket, Toni remembered the waiting taxi.

With burning cheeks, she stammered:

"I'll have to ask you to lend me my taxi-fare please, Mr.—Mr.—"

"Deakes is the name."

"Mr. Deakes. I rushed out of my—my own flat without a coat or bag because I'd been burgled, and I just came here straight to my... my brother. So stupid—leaving my money behind."

Mr. Deakes gave her an interested glance.

"Burgled, were you? Well, I'm not surprised. There's far too many of them 'Ippies and gangs around with their leather jackets and their long hair and all that stuff they learn on the telly about cracking open safes and—"

Toni broke in.

"Forgive me. I *must* pay the taxi."

Mr. Deakes was now more than willing to help the poor pretty young woman. What a story he'd have to tell the Missus when he got back. Fancy the Doctor's sister having to come here, all dressed up for the evening like this and no coat. Scared to death because of them thieves. She looked poorly.

"Mr. Olver will soon get on to the police for you, I know," he said. "Don't you worry, Miss."

He produced the ten shillings she asked for. She paid the taxi driver.

She was thankful when at last the garrulous Mr. Deakes took her up to Nat's flat. He switched on the lights and an electric fire, because he said he thought Miss Olver looked proper cold. Then he departed.

Toni threw herself into a chair and burst into tears. Reaction set in. She had little more fight left in her, and having got this far she could only pray that when Nat did return he would be alone. She must talk things over with him.

Gradually she calmed down, and with some curiosity looked around Nat's sitting room. It had none of the spectacular beauty and luxury of her penthouse but she much preferred its quiet homeliness. There was a big bookcase on the right of the fireplace. Nat, she knew, loved reading. There were no feminine touches; no flower-arrangements and neither was the place particularly tidy. But it was pleasant and comfortable with Victorian furniture and chintz-covered armchairs. The desk by the window was untidily littered with papers. There were one or two paintings on walls which were papered in dark green. One picture in particular Toni remembered from a description Nat had given her—the portrait of a dark-eyed, dark-haired woman with a beautiful but melancholy face. She was wearing a crimson dress. Long slim fingers were clasped together on her lap.

Nat's mother. He had told her how he treasured it. Toni was instantly drawn to that sad Jewish face that had been painted when she was a girl. Nat had her high cheek-bones and tender mouth.

She walked through to Nat's bedroom. It was his all right, she thought. She recognised the blue silk dressing gown thrown over the foot of the bed. It gave her a terrible pang to see it. He had worn it at Mougins. She knew about that tallboy, too. It was Queen Anne walnut and valuable.

On a table by the bed lay a book, a clock and a half-empty packet of cigarettes. There were two filter-tipped ends in the ashtray. She could imagine he had been smoking while he dressed before going out this evening.

Once she had shared a bedroom with Nat, but tonight she felt she had no right in here. She had come unasked. She looked in at the room next door. What she saw there disturbed her; a lot of luggage; a Naval uniform on a hanger outside the wardrobe; a pile of clothes littering the single bed.

Cousin Mervyn must be home.

They were out for dinner and would undoubtedly come back to the flat together.

She thought: *I must get away before they turn up.*

But where to? Never back to Guy. Without money or luggage she could not go to an hotel. And if she applied to any of her friends in London it would be too difficult—because she wouldn't be able to explain her position. She could always appeal to Chris. But she had already been involved. Joe didn't like it.

Toni returned to the sitting room. She found a cigarette and lit it, her fingers shaking.

Before her thoughts could spin round again, she heard Nat's familiar laugh outside the front door. She stood paralysed. Nat and his cousin had come back. She was trapped.

8

Nat was laughing heartily as he walked into the sitting room
—obviously at some shared joke with his cousin. The
laughter died abruptly when he saw the totally unexpected
figure of Toni. He stared at the girl in the grey après-ski suit;
at the white distraught young face that he scarcely recognised.
This ghost of a girl had little in common with the glowing
companion he had brought back from France.

"*Toni!*" he exclaimed and went toward her, both hands
outstretched.

She put hers, cold and trembling, into his long warm fingers.
Over his shoulder she saw Mervyn; not at all like Nat,
shorter, stockier, with the ruddy complexion and watchful
narrow eyes of the sailor.

"I—I'm terribly sorry—" she began, "you must be staggered
to find me here. The porter let me in."

Nat hid what he felt by joking:

"I'll have that fellow on the mat—letting strange women
into my flat. How did you manage it? But of course you'd
get round anyone."

Then he turned to his cousin:

"Mervyn—this is Toni."

Nat's cousin was a man of tact. After shaking hands with
Toni and murmuring something about "being delighted", he
said:

"Forgive me if I buzz off and unpack. Don't think me
rude but my room really is in a shambles."

"Go ahead," said Nat.

The door closed behind Mervyn.

Then Toni was in Nat's arms and they kissed desperately.

"Oh, my darling, *my darling*," Nat kept on saying.

Toni clasped her hands around his neck and pulled his head down to hers again and again. At last she stopped trembling. In his arms things seemed so much better.

He led her to the Chesterfield and sat down.

"What's happened? Why are you here?"

She told her story, leaving out nothing. But she ended by apologising with an insistence that he found pathetic.

"I was so worried about *you* all the time. I didn't mean this to happen. I wanted to avoid it. I went to pieces when Guy first showed me that letter from Ireland. Then that ghastly Leila put the lid on it. She phoned him at the penthouse after dinner. Of course she *knew* I wouldn't want Guy to hear about me being with you in Cannes. She knew it would mean trouble for me and couldn't care less. I think she's always had a 'thing' about Guy though God knows why any woman should. But she didn't like it, so I've been told, when he married me. She always counted on him as her 'extra man'. He was even sort of looked on as her 'boy-friend'—so rumour has it. That's why she wanted to ditch me, I suppose."

"So Guy knows for certain now that you were in Cannes with a man called Gray and that you were *not* with Chris and Joe."

"Yes."

"But he doesn't actually know who Mr. Gray is?"

"No, but the ghastly thing is that he'll soon find out. I suppose once he knows the dates, and what with passports and lists of passengers on air-flights, etc., etc., he could ferret it all out."

"But he might not find it too easy to link the name Gray with Olver," said Nat.

"I hope not," she said miserably.

He looked at her intently.

"Let me get you a drink, darling. You're all in."

She held him back.

"No, don't leave me. Just stay close. I don't want a drink."

"All right, darling."

"I'm afraid I had to borrow from the porter to pay my taxi," she said irrelevantly with a brief laugh.

"What does *that* matter."

"He thinks I'm your sister. That's what I told him. I thought he wouldn't let me in if I didn't."

"My sister," repeated Nat and now he sat up straight and looked at her, put an arm around her shoulders and kissed the top of her head, "I'm glad you're not. I don't love you like a brother."

"Oh, Nat, have I done the absolutely fatal thing by leaving Guy? It means the game's up, doesn't it? Unless we sit tight and say nothing till tomorrow. Then I could borrow some money from you and go and get a room and a job."

He shook his head.

"Out of the question."

She went on miserably:

"Guy became so venomous, I thought after Leila called up he'd either kill me or keep me locked up or something, so I just panicked and rushed to you. But I do feel awful about it."

Nat took her in his arms again and stroked her hair with passionate eagerness.

"Poor baby, I'm glad you came."

"Baby!" She gave a miserable laugh. "There's nothing much of the baby about me any more, though Guy made it plain to me that I'm often stupid and much too emotional—I'm afraid what I've done proves all those things."

"Rubbish. It proves nothing of the sort. You're just not the tough sort or the kind that can cope with a man like your husband. Darling, you did exactly the right thing in coming to me."

"But I can't stay—" she began.

73

"We'll see about that," he broke in.

Fear returned to her eyes.

"Nat, darling, we must remember that you must *not* be involved—it's absolutely essential."

"That's no longer of any interest. My dear darling Toni, I made my own decision yesterday. I wrote you a long, long letter after I woke up. I hadn't time to finish it but you shall read what there is."

He walked to the bureau, took a sheet of paper from the blotter and handed it to her.

"Yes, read it, my love, I want you to see that what you've done tonight is not responsible for my decision to let Guy divorce you and cite me. I intended to bring it about anyhow."

With gathering excitement Toni started to read the letter.

"My very dearly Beloved,

It's half past six a.m. I've just made myself a cup of tea because I couldn't sleep. I had a vivid dream of you. We were in Mougins on that terrace at Mas Candille. I was showing you the mountains. You broke away from me and threw yourself over the terrace. It gave me a ghastly shock but I woke up before anything else happened. Thank God I didn't see your dead body! It was a nightmare, of course, and they say these sort of things arise from a sub-conscious state of anxiety. Well, I've been worrying about you ever since I let you go. I'd have gone round the bend if I hadn't been fantastically busy at the hospital. I was thankful when old Mervyn turned up because the evenings have been especially bitter picturing you trying to cope with that sadist.

On this particular moring I'm lying in bed remembering all your sweetness and beauty, and the absolute delight of loving and being loved by a woman like yourself. Young you may be and a little immature at times, but I've always found you enchanting. I've never been so keen on the 'I can take care of myself you can't fool me' type of girl. I adored you at

Mougins. I enjoyed your quick bright mind, your sense of humour, your capacity for love. To me you were the perfect companion. I realised to the full what life could mean married to you.

It's taken me a little time to sort myself out, Toni darling, but now I know what I want. I want you, whether it means I am a co-respondent in the divorce or not. You've been an absolute angel trying to save 'my reputation' but it's no longer as important to me as you are. Whatever evolves from the scandal I can still go on practising. Anyhow, darling, to hell with all the difficulties. Just write and tell me that you want to be with me as much as ever, and we'll make our plans. Please, Toni, come to me as soon as you can—I love you so much that—"

Here the letter broke off.

Toni raised her head. Her eyes glittered with tears. She gave Nat a look of intense gratitude.

"Darling, thank you with all my heart. It's wonderful of you—especially to realise you reached this decision before I kicked over the traces and ran to you."

He gave a sigh of relief.

"Then the die's cast."

"But I'm still worried—about my surgeon," she said in a low voice.

"Well, your surgeon is not going to worry about himself. He's going to become *your* doctor in all ways."

She clutched the unfinished letter in her fingers, blinking back the tears. Her fears for Nat seemed to dissolve in the warmth of this great moment when she began to feel at last that her life with Guy was ending. A new one was about to begin with the man she loved so much.

"Oh, if you're sure, *sure*, that you won't regret taking me on," she added.

He held her close.

"I'm quite sure. I shall hold to every word in that letter. The only thing that matters now is you. And don't please worry about my profession. I can weather the storm. A lot of other men in the same position have done it."

"But if *he* doesn't find out—"

"I don't care—let Mr. Brand do what he damn well likes. He can either divorce you for the mythical Mr. Gray or for Mr. Nathaniel Olver. But you are staying with me."

Toni shut her eyes and relaxed. She sat very quietly holding on to him with her cheek pressed against his shoulder. Neither of them spoke for a moment. Nat went on stroking her hair. The room was quiet except for the occasional sound of a car in the road below.

She began to imagine Guy in the penthouse, gnawing at his nails, frustrated and furious, wondering what had happened to her. Suddenly she spoke:

"What do we do now, Nat? I *can't* stay here, you know."

"Tonight at least you can—little sister," he added with a grin that made her smile, too.

"But *how?* Your cousin is in the spare room."

"Wait a minute," said Nat, and vanished.

When he came back he was all smiles again. The gravity and strain had gone from his face.

"Everything's fine. Old Mervyn's going to sleep on the sofa in here. No, don't start arguing, my love. It's quite comfortable and Mervyn is a sailor. He can sleep like a top anywhere. He says you can have his room with the greatest pleasure and please to forgive the shambles."

"It's too much—turning your cousin out of his room, on his first night back, too."

Nat said:

"Darling, he knows the situation. He's very sympathetic."

If Toni had any doubt about that, she was reassured when finally Mervyn Olver joined them. He took her right hand in a warm friendly clasp.

76

"Very happy to meet you, Toni—if I may call you that. Nat wrote me about you. I'm sorry things have boiled up like this. It must be very awkward for you both."

"I'm afraid I'm an awful nuisance—" she began.

"Of course you're not," he broke in, and grinned at her. He added:

"Let me tell you I've never seen such fantastic eyes. *What* a colour!"

Now Toni joined in the laughter and shook her head.

"Oh, these eyes!"

"They get you into a lot of trouble, don't they, darling?" Nat laughed, with her.

"Well, let's have a drink," said Mervyn, "I've got a bottle of bubbly in my room. I brought one back for old Nat. We'll open it right now and celebrate this occasion. I'm sure it *is* an occasion."

Toni and Nat exchanged glances and drew close together. He put an arm around her slender waist.

"Very special," he said.

The warmth and gratitude that Toni was beginning to feel welled up like a flame that seemed to thaw her frozen spirit. Nat, looking at her, thought that she had slipped back into being the Toni of Mougins days—his radiant love.

Mervyn disappeared to fetch his champagne.

Nat said:

"He's great."

"Like you. Oh, Nat, am I *really* to stay here with you tonight?"

"You are, my sweet, and until further notice."

"We'll discuss that tomorrow."

"I shall never let you go back to Guy, so that's settled."

"But you told me Mervyn was going to be home on leave for some time. This *is* his home."

"So he was, but there was a letter waiting for him from a retired Naval friend inviting him to Aviemore (you know, in

Scotland) for some shooting. Apparently he has a lovely old place and hundreds of good acres. Mervyn's very keen. He'll be off tomorrow early in any case so not to worry, Toni, my love."

"Are you sure this isn't being cooked up because of me?"

"I give you my word it's a fact."

"And after that, what do we do?" she asked in a low voice and stared around the room.

* * *

The panic, the hysteria had gone. It had been replaced by a cooler more practical and sensible outlook. Thinking things over, it struck her that not only had she run away from Guy but left everything she possessed in the world. Some of the things in the penthouse, some down in Bray. And she had no money. Guy had never given her an allowance. She used to have to ask him for every penny she spent. He had preferred to pay the bills himself. Perhaps, she thought, keeping the reins on the financial side had made him feel all the more certain he could retain possession of her.

"I've nothing with me," suddenly she said, "absolutely nothing."

"Darling, I can buy you whatever you need. I can afford it. Thank God, I'm not poor. I make a good income. You can go out in the morning and get yourself a trousseau."

Yes, she thought, *he has a good income, but that may only be for the moment. He may have to give up his private flourishing practice because of me.*

But Nat refused to listen to her protests. He was singularly relieved to know that she was with him for good. He felt extraordinarily calm and content.

Mervyn returned. The bottle was opened, and the three of them drank the foaming golden champagne, toasting each other. They discussed the future between them. Mervyn confirmed Nat's announcement that he was off in the morning to Aviemore and she was welcome to his room. He wouldn't be back for at least a fortnight, he said, and then no doubt other arrangements would have been made.

"One has to face up to the facts, my dear girl," he said. "You and my cousin have decided to make your lives together. No doubt there'll be a divorce and eventually you'll marry, so your place is with Nat now."

"Oh, Mervyn!" suddenly Toni exclaimed. "Have I been terrible, letting him in for this? Ought I to have come here tonight? Will I ruin his career—his life? If you say so in all honesty, I'll leave in the morning and never see him again—whether Guy divorces me or not."

Nat opened his mouth to protest but Mervyn got in first.

"Hold on, Toni. Your husband may make these investigations and he'll cite Nat anyhow. The fat'll be in the fire whatever you do. You won't be the sole cause of the 'ruin'—if there is ruin, which I doubt. Nat is just as much to blame as you are."

"Exactly," said Nat. "When we got back from Mougins I didn't want to let her go. She insisted because she was afraid of me losing my darned reputation. Okay—it may be a bad show at first but it'll work out."

Mervyn looked at Toni while he sipped his drink. When he had first heard from Nat about her, he had been surprised and anxious. He had always regarded cousin Nat as an essentially sensible, balanced fellow with a distinguished career ahead of him. It had upset Mervyn to think that he might wreck the boat for the sake of a woman, no matter how attractive.

Now that he had met Toni, he reversed his ideas. He could understand why his cousin had fallen so deeply in love. She was a sweet creature and apart from being exceptionally lovely, she seemed very gentle and not in the least the scheming female Mervyn had feared. There was something about Toni that certainly made a man want to look after her. She was honest and generous, too. That was what he liked most. Willing to take all the blame herself and keep Nat out of it.

"Look, Toni," Mervyn said, "I think it's time you stopped fretting. You both know exactly what you've got to give up in order to be together. So go ahead and be as happy as you can."

"I second that," said Nat.

Toni instinctively held a hand out to Mervyn. He took it and patted it between his own in a fatherly fashion. Then he got up and announced that it was time they all turned in. Toni must be exhausted, and if he was to drive up to Aviemore tomorrow, he wanted some sleep.

They were in agreement. A few minutes later Toni was in the little spare room which Mervyn, used to keeping order in a very small space, had tidied up. She felt as though she had been battered by a storm and was still breathless and confused, but she laughed when Nat came in with a pair of pyjamas.

"Oh, I know you'll drown in these," he smiled, "but it's all I can offer my darling, *darling* Toni."

She clung to him, both arms around his waist.

"Thank you with all my heart. Thank you for giving me such a marvellous welcome."

"Thank God you came to me, my love. Now don't lie awake worrying. Go straight to sleep and tomorrow while I'm working you can go on a shopping spree."

"But I'll have to contact Guy tomorrow, won't I? I mean, he might start asking the police to look for me or something—he's quite capable of telling them that I'm a neurotic or even crazy and that I must have lost my memory or something. I want to avoid that and to let him know that I'm okay but that I just don't intend to go back to *him*. And there are all my things; I left the lot."

Nat thought this over frowning.

"I agree that you don't want him to start a police-hunt. But leave your things. Don't go back to that flat for God's sake. I'll get hold of my solicitor tomorrow and see what there is to be done. I presume you own a few things he *hasn't* given you?"

"Very few," she said. "A few odd books; one or two minor pieces of jewellery that belonged to my mother; a little Victorian Prie-Dieu in my bedroom that Aunt Penelope gave me for a wedding present. Honestly, nothing much else. Guy has bought absolutely everything I've had for ages. That's what I find so hateful. I had nothing of my own and no life of my own, and practically no will of my own, either," she added in a low voice.

Nat held her tightly.

"Forget it. Put him right out of your mind tonight. I want you to sleep. Tomorrow, when you know you'll catch him in— phone the flat but don't tell him where you are. Let's avoid an unpleasant scene round here, in case he comes after you because I can't be here to take care of you. I've got two big operations on tomorrow morning. It's the devil."

"Oh, don't worry, Nat—he can't possibly find out where I am, and I don't think he'll try once I've told him I'm never going back to him. I expect he'll just say he'll divorce me, then set to work to find out who for!"

"No, darling," said Nat quietly, "I intend to write to him tomorrow and tell him precisely who the co-respondent is. There's going to be no more of this hide-and-seek."

"Oh, *Nat*—"

"Ssh," he broke in. "Your little head is just going round and round and we'll get no further. Leave it all to me now. I'll take care of you and the whole situation."

9

It seemed strange to Toni that next morning to go shopping and buy so many new things. She didn't really like spending Nat's money, but she supposed it was what she must learn to do in the future.

It didn't take long to find an inexpensive dress and jacket, some lingerie, a pair of slacks and a pullover, suitable shoes, a warm jacket and scarf, gloves and bag. A cheap plastic one which at once became more dear to her than the expensive leather Hermes models she had left behind.

It all seemed rather ridiculous when she remembered her magnificent wardrobe filled with fabulous clothes. The memory of them, of the awful scenes with Guy—of his repulsive, vicious nature—was enough to make her go cold and feel devoutly thankful she was no longer with him. It delighted her to be able to discard the grey evening outfit she had arrived in last night.

She telephoned Guy as soon as Nat left that morning. There was no reply. She did not want to ring him at the office so she decided to wait until he got home this evening. Knowing his habits she would probably find him in between six and seven.

Back in Nat's flat again Toni changed into the slacks and polo-neck jersey she had just bought. Somehow that outfit made her feel better. She then arranged a bunch of chrysanthemums in Nat's sitting room and busied herself in the small kitchen. She had brought in a cold cooked meal which she intended to have ready so that he need not take her out tonight. She wanted this flat to mean *home* to him. She wanted so passionately to make him happy.

When eventually she heard Guy's voice on the telephone, all her old fears seemed to rush back. It was awful, she thought, the way that voice of his could terrorise her.

"Who is it?" he asked.

She shut her eyes.

"It's—Antonia."

An instant's silence. She could hear heavy breathing, then:

"Don't tell me, my dear, you have at least had the courtesy to reassure me that you have not thrown yourself into the Thames."

"I am with the man I love," she said breathlessly, "and I have no intention of throwing myself into the Thames."

Another silence. Toni braced herself for what was coming.

It came—ugly and insulting.

"You *slut!*"

Her cheeks burned but she carried on now. She was done with weakness.

"Call me what you like. If I could put a name to you, it would be much worse. I want you to know that I do not intend to return to you."

"I see. And may I be privileged to ask where you are and with whom? The mythical Mr. Gray, I presume?"

"You presume right."

"But I don't think that's his real name, is it?"

"You'll know in due course. He's written to you."

"Very decent of him," came Guy's sneering voice. "He must be an excellent fellow. Does he make a habit of removing other men's wives?"

"He did not remove me. I removed myself. It's no good lying any more. I admit everything. I went away with him while you were in Rio. But we agreed not to break up my marriage. I was willing to go on living with you until you started to threaten me and scare me to death. Then I knew I couldn't take it any more. I could see the hopelessness of trying to live with you, Guy. I daresay I could bring an action against you on the grounds of mental cruelty if I tried, but I'd rather you got on with the divorce and save a lot of publicity for all our sakes."

Toni heard him draw a hissing breath.

"We'll see about the publicity."

"What do you mean?"

"The day will come when you might wish you'd never left me."

"You're quite wrong and if you think I want my *things*—I don't! I can manage without them. You can sell everything you ever gave me—every piece of jewellery—all my furs—everything—I never want to see them again. I want to forget I've ever been your wife. And there's nothing I want more than for you to divorce me as quickly as possible."

There came from Guy's throat that low evil chuckle which she had always found so menacing.

"Not so fast. You don't seem to realise that I can make life most unpleasant for you, my dear Antonia, and even more unpleasant for your partner in guilt—whoever he is. I don't take kindly to people who try to steal my possessions."

"That's all I've ever been to you—just a possession."

"I can make life extremely awkward for you both."

"We won't care."

"Oh, yes, you will. Once I know who this man is, I promise you, my dear Antonia, I'll make him wish he'd never fallen for you."

The sweat broke out on her forehead.

"I think you know you deserve what I've done to you, Guy, but I did not deserve what *you* did to *me*."

"Goodbye," he said.

"Guy—" she called his name suddenly, frantic with fear. For one mad moment she even considered asking him to take her back and leave her lover alone. But Guy had gone. She did not try to ring him again.

She sat down feeling sick, white and shaking.

She tried to get on top of her nerves by smoking furiously. She was determined not to let Nat find her in 'a state'. An hour later she was in the hall to welcome him home with a radiant smile.

*   *   *

"Hullo, darling!"

He put down his case—the smart black leather doctor's case—and held her close.

"Terrific to find you here waiting for me—just like my wife."

"I feel like your wife," she said, and as they walked arm-in-arm into the sitting room she made a valiant effort to keep up the cheerful façade.

Nat was delighted with the flowers and the meal she had prepared. It was just what he wanted, he said, to be able to stay at home and not have to go out to a restaurant. And it only made him smile to notice Toni had bought tinned soup, cold ham and salad and cheese. She was not domesticated, and had never had to worry about cooking. Anyway he was feeling a lot better now that his letter to Guy had been posted. First-class mail! Nat thought grimly. Mr. Brand can digest it with his breakfast.

Then Toni told him about the telephone call.

"What exactly does he mean—that he'll make us both rue the day?"

"Oh, he'll be delighted once he hears you're a well-known gynaecologist and that he can make things difficult for you—and for me."

They had finished the meal.

Nat stirred the black coffee Toni had just handed him, and lit a cigarette. She glanced at him a little timidly. She knew that stern withdrawn look of his.

"I hope he can do nothing too awful," she said and put out a hand to him. "You *know* I've never wanted to hurt you."

85

He took her hand and kissed it but remained silent. He was wondering as Toni had done whether she could put in a defence on the grounds of mental cruelty. Yet, of course, if she did and Guy failed to get his divorce, where would they be—he, Nat and Toni? In a poor position. It would be stalemate. They could never marry. No—much as Nat loathed the idea of the publicity, he would put Toni first. He was damned if he was going to let her suffer any more. They would have a few tough months ahead of them, but once it was all over, they could be together without fear, and able to marry and start an entirely new life.

All the same, there was another side to Nat's thinking— the loyalty that belonged to the doctor rather than to the man. He had felt a profound desire ever since Medical School, to help suffering humanity. He particularly valued his work and research at the hospital. He could not imagine being without it.

It was possible that his private practice might suffer marginally through divorce because there were certain General Practitioners who would prefer not to send him their patients while the lights of publicity were focused on him. Certainly until the position had clarified itself he couldn't be sure what might or might not evolve. He could visualise certain unpleasant moments ahead—in particular with people like Lucas-Wright—and one or two of the more stuffy senior surgeons in the hospital. And, of course, with the Board of Governors.

"My God," Nat said aloud, "I refuse to feel all that guilty, Toni. Guy is such a bastard. You've had such a grim time. Don't let him scare you any more. Leave it all to me."

She said nothing. But she knew Guy, and Nat didn't. Whatever Nat said to comfort her, in the depths of her heart she was still afraid.

"Darling," she said suddenly, "you are absolutely sure, aren't you, that Guy couldn't get you struck off?"

"Sure. The G.M.C. only do that to the man who misbehaves

with one of his own patients, or who takes drugs, or prescribes them illicitly, or who has been guilty of negligence, self-advertising, or making false declarations."

"What does *that* mean?"

"Oh, if he gives medical certificates to workers to enable them to skip work when they're not really sick."

Toni gave a sigh of relief.

"Well, you're not guilty of any of those things, so let Guy do his worst."

"Now we must discuss your immediate future, my darling."

"Well, I've decided. I can't stay here after tonight," she said, "I must try to get a job or something so that I can make some money, and keep myself."

"Of course I'll help finance you," he began, "but—"

She broke in.

"Till things are sorted out I refuse to live here, Nat. In fact, the sooner cousin Mervyn comes back the better."

He kissed her, then put her gently away.

His face looked tired and drawn. Her heart sank. Already, she thought, she was being a burden. A responsibility to him. Oh, if only it wasn't *Guy* they were up against!

In his arms that night, nothing in the great world outside their room seemed to matter. Their love, their need of each other was all important. But with morning, after Nat had gone—Toni felt sad and nervous about the future again.

* * *

The weather was quite bright and a little warmer. She was encouraged to go out. She made a sudden decision to visit Aunt Penny.

She found Miss Morgan dusting in the little antique shop which was close to Hampstead Underground. Miss Morgan was alone. She came forward as Toni pushed the door open and the bell tinkled. Toni gave her a quick embarrassed look. Miss Morgan returned it with a chilly stare.

Toni was the first to speak.

"Hullo, Aunt Penny," she said lamely.

"Oh—so it is you, Antonia. Why have you come? I wonder you have the nerve to face me."

Then Toni knew that the news had already trickled through to Miss Morgan. Guy must have telephoned and told her that his wife had left him.

She followed her aunt into the shop; so familiar with that musky odour of old furniture and polish common to most junk-shops. Miss Morgan had few really first-class pieces to sell, and after a quick glance round, Toni noted that she had replaced many of her treasures for cheaper trashy stuff—easier perhaps, in these days, to dispose of.

Aunt and niece faced each other in the small office at the rear of the shop.

Rather sad, Toni thought, that her mother's sister should be so absolutely different from the sweet lovable mother Toni remembered. Aunt Penny had always looked eccentric, and wore what Toni used to call 'arty-crafty' clothes—long home-spun dresses, tasselled scarves. She had a stern, plain face and was tall and stooping. Her one claim to beauty was her thick reddish-brown hair—masses of it, which she wore scraped back from her high forehead and pinned in a bun at the nape of her neck. She pretended to rummage among some papers on her desk for a moment, then lifted her head, took off her glasses and stared at Toni.

"It's a long time since you came to see me," she said, "and of course I know you have never cared whether I lived or died in spite of the fact I brought you up and did so much for you. I've tried to be reasonable and tell myself that now you are married to a wealthy man and have many engagements, I mustn't expect any attention. But things have changed. I object strongly to the step you have taken in leaving your husband for another man. It is absolutely disgraceful, Antonia."

"Would it have been any better if I had left him *not* for

another man but only because I could not stand living with him any more?"

Miss Morgan tossed her head. A hairpin fell out of her hair. She stooped, thrust it in again with a vicious stab.

"I'm not prepared to argue. Anyhow there *is* another man. Poor Guy told me. He's most terribly upset and I think you are just as you always were—a complete egotist. You *couldn't* have thought one bit about Guy's feelings or you would never have hurt him so dreadfully."

Toni listened to this in silence but with a slightly cynical twist of the lips. She said:

"His vanity may be hurt—nothing else. Don't imagine I've broken his heart, Aunt Penny. He hasn't got one."

"Nonsense. You are trying to put yourself in the right. Guy has never been anything but most generous to you from the word go. You've been thoroughly spoilt by him. You'd been spoilt by your mother when you first came to me as a young girl."

Toni tried to be patient. It was the old Aunt Penny, so free with her criticisms, her complete lack of understanding. She, Toni, hadn't been at all spoilt when she was a child.

It was several years now since Toni had walked out of her aunt's home where she had found no affection, no happiness.

"Aunt Penny," she said, "do you think anyone really knows what goes on between husband and wife once they are alone?"

"You can't alter my private opinion with clever-clever talk. I'm not a fool. Guy has been a wonderful husband. You are just trying to justify your adultery."

Toni turned away and looked for a moment through the back window into a sordid yard where a lean cat was rubbing its back against a garbage pail. She felt desperately depressed. She hadn't expected to find sympathy here but the fact that Aunt Penny sympathised so completely with Guy and possessed not a shred of feeling for her, did nothing to cheer her.

She sighed deeply.

"You obviously want to blame me. I can only assure you Guy is schizophrenic and not what he appears to you. He shows one side to the world, and another to me. My private life with him was absolutely miserable. And at times revolting."

Miss Morgan stared at her niece's back.

"What do you mean? How could it have been revolting?"

"I couldn't possibly explain and I won't try, but I must at least be fair to myself and say it is not all my fault that our marriage hasn't worked out. If you want to think it is, I can't help it."

"And what about this other man?"

"He's a surgeon, actually, and a marvellous man. He fell in love with me and I adore him. I want Guy to divorce me. That's all."

"Absolutely disgraceful!"

"Aren't you a bit out of date, Aunt Penny? Divorce may not be desirable but it is no longer *disgraceful*."

"That's a matter of opinion. I shall never approve of the permissive behaviour of you young people today. It would have been different if your husband had given you real cause for your misconduct."

"That," said Toni, tight-lipped, "is something you know nothing about and you don't want to know. I'd better go."

Miss Morgan looked her niece up and down. The girl's pallor—an unusually drawn look around the strangely beautiful eyes roused sudden pity in her. She was a woman of strict principles but not inhuman. This was her own sister's child, her flesh and blood. In a kinder voice she said:

"I'm sorry, Antonia. You and I have never got on. I deplore your action in leaving Guy no matter what the reason. But it's your life, not mine. I don't suppose you expect me to give you a home till the divorce is over."

"No, I don't."

Miss Morgan looked relieved, then she said:

"I take it for granted Guy will sue you and this man immediately."

"You can be sure he'll do all he can to make things awkward for Nat."

"Nat," calmly repeated Miss Morgan, staring at her niece over her horn-rims, "so that's the name of your surgeon. I have nothing but contempt for a medical man who does what he has done. You're leaving a good man for a bad one."

Toni went scarlet, then resisting the temptation to defend Nat, she turned away from her aunt's malicious gaze.

"Goodbye, Aunt Penny, I'm sorry I came, and you can be quite sure I did *not* intend to stay."

Miss Morgan's voice followed her out of the shop:

"Of course if you're ever in real need, Antonia; I am, after all, your aunt—"

But Toni had shut the door behind her. The little bell tinkled, and was silent. She walked down the familiar road toward the Underground. She felt a little sick. She had not expected sympathy from her aunt but the encounter had been very unpleasant and she realised suddenly how absolutely alone she was now in the world—except for Nat. The hateful implications against him upset her. How many other people beside Aunt Penny would misunderstand—be contemptuous of him and side with Guy? And Nat was not the despicable cad Aunt Penny called him.

But I can't argue like that, Toni told herself wretchedly, *Nat and I have both done wrong in the eyes of the world. A lot of people won't mind but a lot will. Oh, God, God, don't let things be too bad for Nat. Don't, God—please don't!*

IO

That same evening in Nat's flat, the atmosphere was a little less enchanted than it had been the night before. Nat came home looking exhausted.

"Oh, darling," Toni said, "you're all in."

"No—I'm fine. How's yourself, my honey?"

She did not let his attempt at flippancy deceive her and persisted:

"Something horrid has happened to upset you?"

"Tell me how *you've* got on." He, too, persisted, anxious not to distress her.

While they drank their sherry, sitting on the sofa in the sitting room, Toni told him her news. She glossed over the disagreeable meeting with her aunt, then said that she had later in the afternoon seen Chris to tell her what had happened. Chris was terribly sorry, in fact quite devastated after all her efforts to back Toni's alibi. But she thought a divorce in the end would be the best thing. Chris *knew* about Guy and what he could be like. She wanted Toni to leave him. Especially as there were no children to consider.

"Joe himself suggested that I should go and stay with them while things are as they are. I might do so for a few weeks anyhow."

Nat leaned forward, cigarette between his lips.

"Stay here with me—to hell with publicity," he said. His eyes were unhappy.

"No, I mustn't. Actually I've fixed it up with Chris. I move to Ovington Gardens tomorrow."

"What?" He looked upwards swiftly at the young lovely face. Now, whenever he saw Toni or thought about her, he found it strange—even difficult—to believe that the girl who had originally been introduced to him as a millionaire's wife, was now *his*—to love, to protect, and to marry when the whole sordid business was over.

She was telling him about Chris and Joe's maisonette. Ground floor and basement, with a tiny garden at the rear which they found useful for the child. They had one small spare bedroom next to the kitchen. It was dark but it was comfortably furnished. Chris had apologised but it was the only thing she could offer her friend.

"I'm perfectly happy about it," she told Nat.

"I'm not," he muttered. "You in a basement bed-sitter— that's a bit much. You're used to the lap of luxury."

"If you think I shall miss the penthouse or Bray, you're mistaken. I'm off to my bolt-hole tomorrow and I'm free to come and see you or you can come to me whenever we want. Besides, Chris thinks she can find me a temporary job."

"Oh, for God's sake," said Nat loudly, "there's no need for that. I'm not a poor man."

"When I'm living with you, you can spend your money on me but not yet, darling. If I need help I'll ask for it. Chris has a friend who runs a super hairdressing salon not far from Harrods. The owner is French. He married a girl called Madge something-or-other—a distant cousin of Chris's. She phoned this woman and she said they'd give me at least a living wage to help the juniors with shampooing and so on. They're so short of staff. I might even do it for months, Nat. I like hairdressing—it might prove useful to learn a trade. I've done nothing so far but be an *au-pair* girl in Paris where unfortunately I met Guy. The owner of the salon, Yves Bertrand, spoke to me personally. He sounds charming and said I'd be particularly useful with my fluent French, as they have a number of Continental clients."

Nat listened to all this in gloomy silence. Toni had not been deceived by his gay greeting, and he was not deceived now by her bright pleased voice. He knew perfectly well that she did not really care for the idea of being a hairdresser's assistant when only a few days ago she would have been received as a valuable client.

Toni saw Nat's expression and took one of his hands between her own.

"Enough about me, darling. What's your news?"

"Guy got my letter and sent his reply by hand to my consulting room."

"Oh, lord, what does he say?" Toni asked dismally.

"I don't know. It was not really for me. The envelope inside is addressed to you. Here it is."

Nat took it out of his case and threw it on to her lap. She stared at the all too well-known writing. Guy had a large rather feminine hand with a lot of loops and flourishes. She hated seeing it. The very name *"Antonia"* scrawled across the envelope was far too reminiscent of him.

Her heartbeats accelerated as she drew out three sheets of heavy cream paper with the penthouse address, and read what Guy had written.

At the end she looked up, her face stony, then handed the letter to Nat.

Nat took it. It was unpleasant and menacing. Only what Nat might have expected.

"My dear Antonia,

I received Mr. Olver's letter this morning. It was no shock to me, of course, although I did, in fact, find myself shocked that a medical man of his repute should have sunk so low as to entice a wife away from her home.

I can only suppose he takes it for granted that the scandal of such a divorce as ours will have no effect upon his status. In due course he may learn otherwise.

It is by a singular coincidence that the day after you so stupidly ran out of the flat to join your paramour, I lunched with Rupert Sydell, an old friend of my father's; in fact, they were at school together. Sydell is, as Mr. Olver will inform you, Chairman of the Board of Governors of the Royal Queenbury Hospital. He informed me that they were in dire need of funds, like most big hospitals. He was deeply grateful when I offered to make them a generous gift. I gave him a cheque there and then for twenty thousand pounds. He couldn't thank me enough. It has also been suggested that in the near future I might be invited to join the Board.

Your Mr. Olver is a consulting gynaecologist at this hospital and much thought of. Little doubt he is excellent at his job but when I tell Lord Sydell what his morals are like, I doubt very much whether he will be looked upon with quite so much approval . . . at least by the Governors."

At this point Nat stopped reading. His face had gone a dusky red. Every muscle in his body tautened.

God, he thought, *God! Brand calls it a "singular coincidence". Singular it is. Too damned singular. He's thought it all out.*

"What is it?" Toni asked with a handkerchief pressed to her lips, although she guessed which part of the letter he had reached. That story about Lord Sydell horrified and dismayed her. Of course she, too, guessed that it was a diabolical move on Guy's part to make things awkward for Nat—not genuine charity that had led Guy to offer that handsome donation.

Nat continued to read.

"However, my dear Antonia, I am nothing if not magnanimous and I am still reluctant to part with you. Despite the fact that you had behaved so badly, I am willing to lower my pride and bring this whole unhappy matter to a conclusion if you agree to return to me immediately. On the understanding, of course, that you will never see Mr Nathaniel Olver again.

If you consent, I will never mention his name to you again nor to Lord Sydell, at any time. We will hush up the whole affair. I can deal with Leila. I will also guarantee to do my level best to make you happier in the future than you have been in the past.

I would like an immediate answer to this. I shall be out tonight but please call the flat before ten o'clock tomorrow morning.

I warn you that if you decide to stay with Olver, I shall not only tell Sydell the full facts but sue for a divorce, also ask for heavy damages against Olver for enticement, etc.

The final decision lies with you. I wish to have no communication whatsoever with Olver. In my opinion he is beneath contempt."

Toni looked up with a feeling of despair at Nat's face. It was now convulsed with anger. All too well she remembered the final words: *Beneath contempt.* Exactly what Aunt Penny had said, and it wasn't true. But how many other people would second the condemnation—mainly because Nat was in the medical profession—and knowing none of the facts. And as for Guy's promise to "make her happier"—he couldn't—no matter what he did.

Nat said in a cool curt voice.

"So that's that. We're in for it, my darling. Pretty damnable. How the hell could we expect that *your* husband would play financial benefactor to *my* hospital."

Toni sprang to her feet.

"Guy knew about us before he lunched with Sydell. I'll swear to that. I've never heard him mention the Royal Queenbury. We hardly know the Sydells, we just joined them once at a Charity Ball Lady Sydell had organised."

"I'll tell you what he's like," said Nat grimly, "there's a line in a poem by Flint about just such a man: *'Oh, Primrose*

96

of respectability, ward, and warden of the Church. As you go home ... the tradesmen do you homage. Happily the trees do not know you.' That describes Sydell. He's known at the Royal Queenbury as an old humbug. He sits in judgment on everyone but himself. But he's the Chairman and good at raising funds for the hospital so what he says goes."

"He *would* be an old friend of Guy's father," exclaimed Toni.

Nat put the letter down on the table.

"I tell you he's manœuvred *this*," Toni added. "I know Guy inside-out. He must have looked you up, found out which hospital you were at, then quickly asked his Lordship to lunch. As for the donation, Guy is a snake. He'll spend a fortune if he wants to get his own back on us."

"On me, you mean. He still seems to want you, my poor darling."

Toni stared at Nat, speechlessly. That horrible letter of Guy's had brought all the coldness and cruelty of his nature into this warm room where they had found so much happiness.

Nat drank his second sherry slowly, thoughtfully. His own thoughts were chaotic. Once Lord Sydell and his colleagues got wind of this thing, he, Nat, would be privately if not publicly censored by quite a few of the high-ups at the Royal Queenbury. The divorce case would, in certain quarters, be regarded as a slur upon his character and thus reflect on his hospital. It might even lead to him being asked to resign.

Such a possibility seemed suddenly to lower Nat's whole morale. He could judge from Guy Brand's letter the extent to which the man was prepared to go to take his revenge. It wasn't a pretty prospect.

Nat walked to Toni and took her in his arms. She was crying. He said:

"Don't, my darling—don't let this get you down. It *is* a nasty blow but we'll get over it. And we can't glorify our behaviour. Let's be realistic. The co-respondent generally appears as a contemptible fellow, if you think about it. Guy has the right to object to his wife being taken away from him."

Toni sobbed:

"I wasn't taken away. I came to you of my own accord."

"I took you away. Full stop!"

"He deserved it and you *aren't* contemptible! You aren't. You aren't. *You aren't.*" Toni choked over the denial.

He smiled down at her with tender gratitude. His spirits revived in the warmth and sincerity of her love.

"Dearest, even today when divorce means so little, I shall be labelled a bastard by the world around us."

"Only a small proportion."

"Unfortunately it's the half that can make things bloody difficult for us both," said Nat with a curt laugh.

"It isn't fair. Nobody knows how the generous charitable Guy Brand behaves in his own home—particularly in the bedroom."

Nat grimaced.

"Dearest, nobody knows what goes on in anyone else's bedroom—and seldom sees them as they really are. Didn't someone once say: *'If the world could see me as I really am, not a soul on earth would pity me'?*"

She raised a wet indignant face and even in this grim moment, Nat thought how beautiful her eyes were—and how small and soft and defenceless she was—his poor little Toni.

"*Everybody* would pity us!" she cried hotly, "that's a horrid quotation, Nat."

"Darling, let's face it, the die's cast. Let Guy get on with his venomous spite."

She drew away from Nat, shaking her head.

"No—I won't allow it."

"You can't stop it—" began Nat, then with sudden understanding, gripped both her arms and looked at her angrily. "Oh no, don't run away with the idea that you can go back to him just because he's offered you the chance."

"I would go back. I *will* too, if he'll swear to leave you alone, and he says he will if he can get me back. He just can't bear to let everyone we know think he's been *left*. That's why he's putting up a fight to keep me."

"And what do you take me for?" Nat snapped. "Do you think I'd accept any favours from him, my dear? After what he's done to you? Oh no, get it right out of your head that I'll let you go back. If you go, I'll follow you and I'll spill the whole story to Lord Sydell myself, and to the hospital. Then they'll know about us anyhow and your sacrifice will be useless. Understand, Toni, you're not to be made a martyr for my sake. Guy can do what he damn well likes. We'll weather it. He may make it a bit difficult but we want that divorce, and we want him to get it, and we're going to be married as soon as it's all over. So there's an end to it."

She made no reply. She cried stormily. They clung together now as though for moral rather than for physical support, and tried to comfort each other.

It could not be said that they had a happy evening although they cooled down finally, and talked things over more calmly. Nat, warming in a blaze of optimism, announced that he could not really see that his position at the hospital would be jeopardised, no matter how friendly Guy was with Lord Sydell. Nat had many friends there and it was no exaggeration to say that the world *had* changed, and although he agreed that moral rectitude was to be desired, a man could lapse without incurring the harsh inflexible condemnation of the Victorians.

"Mind you, I'm not trying to justify what we did, darling," he added, "but we both had out eyes wide open when we went to France."

Toni sat silently remembering what Guy could be like when he was denied anything that he wanted. How hateful—

and malicious he could be behind that mask-like charm—
especially when he was thwarted.

She shuddered at the remembrance.

When she said goodbye to Nat that next morning she had
the sudden panic-stricken sensation that she was going a long
way away from him. She held on to him, trying to keep her
self-control. No matter how much she wanted to cry—and
tears came easily to Toni—she meant to resist such weakness
from now onward. She was quite sure weeping women irritated
the average man—even Nat.

"See you," she said in a muffled voice and hid her face
against his shoulder. "Ring me up at Chris's tonight if you
can. There won't be any new development, of course, because
Guy's waiting for my reply."

Nat glanced at his wrist watch.

"It's only just after nine. Are you going to ring him?"

"Yes, after you go."

He drew in a whistling breath.

"I wish to God I could stay and help you through it but
I've got an urgent appointment—I'm late now. I *must* see a
patient I operated on yesterday."

"Go ahead. I'm okay. I've got to learn to be a surgeon's wife,
haven't I?" Toni managed a laugh.

He picked up his case, tugging at his collar as though it
was too tight for him.

"Quite sure you *want* to tell Guy you won't go back?"

"Absolutely."

*   *   *

After Nat had kissed her goodbye and gone, Toni walked
into the bedroom, sat down on the bed and lifted the telephone-
receiver. She had to confess to herself that she felt frightened.
It was usual for Guy to have that effect on her. But she went
ahead—fortified by the memory of Nat and of their mutual
love. Besides, her very flesh crawled at the mere thought of

what she might have to endure if she *did* go back to Guy.

As soon as he answered her call she told him categorically that she hadn't the slighest intention of returning to him.

"You are quite sure, Antonia? You realise to the full what I intend to do if you persist in this folly?"

"As far as I'm concerned it isn't folly. I love Nat and I shall be very happy with him and he feels the same about me."

"You're worse than a fool," came Guy's voice again, this time on a low furious note. She could visualise his face; the ugliness of his mean mouth; the glacial stare of those light grey eyes which could so quickly reduce her to a state of nerves. But this time she wasn't going to be defeated.

"You're more stupid than I ever thought you," he went on, "And as for loving this man who's taken you on, you're a hypocrite. You can't care a damn about him, otherwise you wouldn't want to wreck his life."

The moisture broke out on the palms of Toni's hands.

"He won't be ruined," she said. "That's only what you think. I am not a patient of his, he couldn't be struck off by the G.M.C. As for your low-down cunning behaviour with Lord Sydell—Nat's prepared to face up to the consequences."

A moment's silence. Then Guy said in an odd sort of voice, she thought:

"We shall see."

"Well, how *can* he be ruined as I was not a patient of his?" Toni protested again.

"*Weren't you?*"

Just for an instant she was taken aback. What did he mean by that? What fresh evil was he cooking up? He was really a reptile, she thought. His fangs were deadly.

Then she managed a laugh.

"You know perfectly well I wasn't, Guy."

"I have no time to argue about it, Antonia, but I warn you again that the final decision rests with you. You played a dirty trick on me while I was in Rio. All that pretence you put up of being in Ireland—that innocent role of the misjudged wife makes me sick."

"You drove me to it, Guy. I'd never have been unfaithful to you if you'd treated me kindly."

"I denied you nothing."

"Except kindness and consideration and even common decency at times," she said with rising passion. "And what about you—*your* hypocrisy—acting the perfect husband in public. I wonder how you'd like your friends—including the Sydells—to hear how you often behaved when we were alone. It's not surprising I fell for a man like Nat. Please, Guy, just divorce me, then leave us alone."

He was silent. Toni's face twitched nervously. Then he said:

"I intend to leave *you* alone. But if it is possible for me to put an end to your so-called 'good man's' medical career, I intend also to do just that."

"How can you be so fiendish?" she cried indignantly. "You're a devil full of cunning. You gave that cheque to Sydell only after you found out that the Royal Queenbury was *Nat's* hospital. Only *you* could have thought up such a vile plan."

Guy let that sink in, then she heard that wicked chuckle she used to dread.

"Believe me, my dear, I can think up some still worse things," he drawled. "However, it's up to you."

"I won't come back to you," Toni cried, her control slipping. "*I won't*, and you can keep all my things too, except those my own mother left me. I don't want anything *you* ever gave me. And I'm not scared of you, Guy. You can't do anything to Nat except cite him as a co-respondent. He's quite prepared to accept that. So don't threaten me."

"Poor little kitten, you're easily scared," came his sneering voice, "What a pity you want to ruin your own life as well as Mr. Olver's. You won't be happy with him as time goes on, you know. He won't thank you for all the publicity and embarrassment he'll have to suffer, or if his work goes down-hill, or even comes to a fullstop. He'll soon grow tired of your lily-white body and wish he'd never set eyes on you."

"That's a lie! Oh, I hate you, Guy. I shall hate you till I die."

And now she slammed down the receiver. She was trembling violently. She couldn't cope with Guy any longer. He had the unholy power of making her feel stupid and almost speechless. She felt that her very vitals were being churned up by his deliberate cruelty. For some time she sat on the edge of the bed with her face in her hands. No doubt most of his threats were empty. But he had said enough to destroy what little peace was left to her. What had he meant by querying the fact that she had not been a patient of Nat's? It could only be an idle threat. But it made her uneasy. Neither was she able to forget his final warning. *"He won't thank you once he's grown tired of your lily-white body and his work goes downhill. He'll end by wishing he'd never set eyes on you."*

She wouldn't dare repeat those brutal horrible words to Nat. It would enrage him. Besides, she didn't even want him to consider such a possibility. It had never entered *her* head that —in time—he would ever resent her because of the divorce.

She packed a few belongings and made ready to go to Ovington Gardens. Before she left Nat's flat she stood staring wretchedly at the telephone.

Almost she picked up the receiver to re-dial Guy's number. Almost she decided to tell him she had thought over the whole situation, and wished to go back to him at once. Then she imagined what Nat might feel if she did such a thing. He'd be demented. He loved her as much as she loved him. He had told her a dozen times last night. Now, emotionally torn to pieces, Toni looked at the ring he had slipped on her marriage finger last night. A small but charming topaz set in twisted gold.

"It isn't valuable, my love, but the stone is the colour of

your eyes," he had said. "It belonged to my mother. I have kept it for my future wife."

Nat was not the sort of man to make such a gesture if he hadn't been absolutely sure of his love for her. She could not walk out on him—either for his sake or her own.

But the idea Guy had so devilishly implanted in her mind continued to torment Toni. She stayed on in the flat in a state of indecision and misery, walking up and down, trying to shut out the memory of Guy's malicious words.

Finally she left Nat's flat and joined Chris. Once there she poured out the whole story to her friend. Chris was a practical girl, less emotional than Toni. She jeered at Guy's veiled insinuations.

"He was just being his usual beastly self. He can't possibly ruin Nat. Do stop being so afraid of him. Obviously Lord Sydell won't be pleased, but in these days people gloss over divorce. Besides they know how valuable Nat is to them in the hospital. As for that prig, Mr. Lucas-Wright, if he turns nasty, it will be simple enough for Nat to find another surgeon to share a consulting room with. Of *course*, a few eyebrows will be raised over him running away with you, darling, and the odd unpleasant person might avoid him, and all that, but I believe Guy is just trying to scare you into going back to him."

"Oh, Chris—" Toni caught hold of her friend's hand and pressed it, "you don't honestly think Nat could turn against me one day?"

"Idiot—of course not. Look here, you're absolutely exhausted—you can't think straight. Let's go into the kitchen. I'll make you a strong cup of coffee, then maybe I'll take you round to see my friend Madge, at Bertrands. You'll feel better when you've fixed up that job. Do stop worrying, will you, please?"

Toni shut her eyes, opened them again wearily, but found it possible to smile.

"Okay. I must say you do boost my morale, Chris, and perhaps you're right. Darling, what *would* I have done without you?"

"I'm afraid I haven't been much of a success really. Joe and I both feared from the start that you were taking a frightful risk."

"But you know I don't care we've been found out—as far as I am concerned. I'm so terribly relieved to be away from Guy. Nat's my worry."

II

One damp foggy morning in early October, Guy Brand stood in the crowded lounge of the Cumberland Hotel looking smug and handsome as usual, wearing a smart grey Burberry and carrying gloves and a small attaché case.

He could never actually remember having been in this hotel before. It was not one of his haunts. But he had decided that it was much the safest place for him to meet the young woman he had asked to lunch as it was almost one hundred per cent certain that nobody he personally knew would come here and recognise him.

He glanced again at a letter he had just taken from his pocket. It was from a Private Investigation Bureau—an excellent one. He was paying them well. There was nothing now that he did not know about Nathaniel Olver. And the girl he was about to entertain—Olver's secretary, Miss Teresa Withers.

The letter also contained many important pieces of information about Miss Withers' private life. What Guy was concerned with now was the description of her. Having digested this, he replaced the letter in his case.

With his large cold grey eyes searching the crowd that milled in and out of the popular hotel, he recognised Teresa as soon as she walked in. There she was, just as described, plumpish figure, sallow skin, rather oily dark hair dressed in a high chignon, big dark eyes. Not attractive and palpably of foreign blood.

Guy was never embarrassed. He walked up to her and said with a smile:

"Miss Withers?"

She looked a trifle startled but nodded and smiled.

"Yes. I suppose you're Mr. Brand."

"Well met," he said pleasantly. "What a wretched day it is. I expect you'd like a drink. I know I would."

"It would be great," said Teresa, who liked her drinks and could not afford to buy as many as she wished. She had to scrape a few pounds out of her salary every month in order to buy Rod, her boy-friend, the vodka he favoured.

Guy suggested that they should go straight to the Grill Room and order drinks there because he hadn't too much time and he was sure, he said, that she would want to get back to her own work.

This being agreed upon, they faced each other at a corner table. Guy ordered a light sherry for himself and a vodka and lime for his guest. She had learned to like that, whereas before she had met Rod she had never touched a drop of alcohol. But she had changed completely since she fell for Rod, and set up housekeeping with him.

Remembering the flat—the continual disorder and noise— because Rod filled it with his friends from the Film or T.V. Studios and she never had time to clean it up—Teresa appreciated the prospect of being treated to a good lunch. This had really been a blind date for her. Mr. Brand had merely telephoned and asked her if she could meet him for lunch on a matter of great urgency. He had also asked her to keep the invitation under her hat, as the matter he was about to discuss was very personal.

Teresa had been intrigued. She was not the sort of girl who received many invitations and little or no promise of such excitement. Who on earth *was* Mr. Brand? Why should he want to give her lunch at the Cumberland? Well, she'd soon find out!

Meanwhile she enjoyed her vodka and sat looking at her

host with some admiration. He was terribly good-looking and smart, she thought, although a bit gross, perhaps, and a bit old-fashioned. She liked men thin like Rod. And Rod was very modern with his long hair and side-burns and gay shirts and jackets. But what a beautiful voice Mr. Brand had, and he was very much the gentleman. When Teresa first fell for Rod, eighteen months ago, he had had a nice voice, too, but had lately adopted a psuedo-American twang. If she wanted to talk to him when he was otherwise occupied, he'd say things like *"Beat it, kid,"* or threaten to *"take her to the cleaners"* if she didn't fall in with all that he wanted. She didn't really know why she put up with him except that she was so desperately in love. And except for an insipid, abortive affair she'd had while she was still at Pitman's College, at the beginning of her career, she had never had a man mad about *her* before. She was desperately sex-hungry when she met Rod. He'd gone for her and for the first and only time in her life she was fulfilled. If at any time she found it a burden to have to spend most of her salary on him—for his jobs were few and far between and he wasn't too generous with his pay when he got it—she always found excuses for him. He couldn't help it. It wasn't his fault that good jobs for actors were hard to come by and when she really got upset with him, he made up for it. He was terrific in bed and made her feel a real woman at last. She was sure that even though he was a few years younger than herself, he'd marry her one day. He'd promised. Meanwhile she was more than happy to live with him.

It wasn't until the lunch had been ordered—smoked salmon and steaks—an improvement on Teresa's usual cheap sandwich and glass of milk—that she began to realise what this meeting was about.

* * *

She gasped a little when Mr. Brand told her.

"Nothing of course is in the papers yet and I don't suppose Mr. Olver has told you a thing," he said, "but he has enticed my wife away from me. I am suing him for divorce."

Teresa took off her horn-rim spectacles and blinked her long eyelashes—the false ones she was wearing for the occasion.

"*Wow!*" she exclaimed, "I can't believe it."

Guy tapped his lips with his table napkin.

"It's perfectly true and you will soon be reading a full account of it. Mr. Olver and I are both men with considerable reputations in the country, so the divorce will not go unnoticed, I assure you."

"Well, I *never!*" said Teresa lamely, and made a little blowing sound of disbelief.

Guy looked at her with distaste. He hated swarthy women and especially plump ones with greasy skins, but he had only the kindliest smile for Teresa whom he was going to turn into his most valuable ally in the battle he was waging against her employer.

"So it hasn't reached your ears yet?" he murmured.

"Not a word, but Mr. Olver is never very talkative except about his work and he's always in a rush."

"And you've never heard the name Mrs. Guy Brand—Antonia, more often than not called 'Toni'?"

"Never."

"Very discreet of Mr. Olver," said Guy with his bland smile. "So I am right in thinking that my wife was not a patient of Mr. Olver's?"

"No, she's never consulted him to my knowledge and I've been through the books recently and she's not on his list."

Guy put his tongue in his cheek and continued to eat his smoked salmon. By the time the steaks had come and been consumed, Teresa knew quite a bit more about Nathaniel Olver and this gentleman's *wife*. *Wow*, she said to herself again, what a thing! She'd never have thought it of Mr. Olver. She'd found him very attractive—most women did—but certainly not sexy toward her or any of the women who came to consult him. He was most circumspect and she was always present during his examination of his patients. Apart from that, she would never have thought him the type to go for another man's wife. So dangerous for a fellow in his profession. But it appeared that he had actually taken this girl Antonia away for a whole week in the South of France.

Guy completed his story and leaning across the table looked at Teresa with an expression of deep sorrow.

"You can imagine how I feel," he said.

"Oh, I think it's ghastly for you, and you're so nice... I mean you seem so nice," she corrected herself a little confusedly. "And I just can't get over Mr. Olver doing such a thing to you. I never thought he'd be such a heel. I tell you I'm *flabbergasted!*"

Guy sighed.

"You see how mistaken one can be in people. I was equally mistaken in my wife in whom I had perfect trust and have always treated with the utmost generosity."

"Come to think of it," said Teresa, "I've been cudgelling my brains all through this meal about the name Guy Brand. Of course I've seen it in the Glossies and the Gossip Columns. You're very well known and your wife's a great beauty. I've seen photographs of you both at parties and dances—in Naussau and Bermuda, on water-skis and that sort of thing. And she has a famous emerald ring, hasn't she? I read about that."

"Yes, I gave her all I could and did everything to make her happy."

"God, some girls never know when they're well off."

"And you, Miss Withers—or let me call you Teresa—you're not particularly well off, are you?"

"How do you know?" she stared at him.

"Oh, I know quite a bit. I always make it my business to find out about the people I make friends with," he said suavely.

She gave a short laugh.

"Well, I can't say I often have a meal like this. I used to—

when things were better in my life although I've had a bit of a hard time from the start. My parents are dead and I was actually adopted but I didn't get on with the couple who adopted me and—"

Guy allowed her to whine and complain for quite a few minutes about her hard life. It pleased him. It was exactly what he wanted—somebody who was really in need of money. And it was obvious from what Miss Teresa Withers was saying that it was the lack of money that made life so difficult for her now, even though she got a good salary as secretary-receptionist to a well-known gynaecologist. Most of the money went on the cost of living, she said.

Guy knew, having digested all the notes sent to him by his Investigator, that she was living with a boy-friend. The Investigator had done well. Ferreted out a lot about the background of the pair. He had haunted the little pub two doors up from the flat Teresa and Rod shared. It appeared that Rodney spent a lot of time with Teresa in this pub and they had a crowd of hard-drinking and some of them *drugging* friends. In fact Mr. Olver's receptionist who was so efficient, clean and good at her job, was quite a different person once she got home. There she was much more 'with it', her long black hair hanging around her neck (so the Investigator described it) and wearing gay slacks and tunics and gold chain belts. Various gossips had also told the detective she was crazy about her boy-friend and was keeping him.

Poor wretch, Guy reflected, but without real pity because it suited him that Teresa should be leading such a sordid life. She might so easily have been unapproachable and quite the wrong person to accept the bribe he wanted to offer—for reasons he was about to unfold. Once having made up his mind to go to any length to revenge himself on Nathaniel Olver and Antonia who would obviously suffer with Nat, Guy was prepared to act without scruple.

He plied Teresa with more vodka and plenty of sympathy,

and finally asked her whether she was really and truly in love with this boy—Rodney Best.

Teresa, dusky-red, smoked the cigarette Guy had just lit for her with her coffee, and bluntly confessed that she was "mad about Rod" and that he was her whole life.

"Sometimes he plays me up but we get on very well in the ways that matter," she said meaningly, "and it's only because we can't afford to create an impression that he hasn't got on as an actor. I mean, what he needs is a smart flat where we can entertain the film chaps and cut a figure and ply everybody with drinks, and then he'd get right into the studios instead of hanging round the pub as he has to—waiting for work—poor Rod."

Guy nodded. Teresa's troubles bored him to death but he was alert to the need to humour her. Suddenly he said:

"And what would *you* do to a woman who took your Rodney away from you if the occasion arose?"

Teresa's eyes flashed. Her lips took an ugly twist.

"I'd want to *kill* her—I'd do anything to get my own back."

"So would I," said Guy lightly.

But she caught the full meaning of the expression in his eyes and realised that this man had a deep dark side. He could be vindictive, of that she was sure. She drank her coffee and greedily chewed a spoonful of the sugar crystals left in the cup.

"I ought to be dieting," she said with a stupid laugh, "instead of munching sugar."

"You should go to a place like Buxted or Forest Mere Hydro where I'm thinking of going in order to get my weight down," said Guy, still watching her closely.

"Ooh, I wish I could. Rod's always telling me I'm too fat."

"You'd be very attractive if you were a little slimmer, if I may say so, and could wear the sort of clothes my wife used to like."

"Oh, I'm no beauty like her. I remember her photographs."

Guy's fingers interlocked under the table, and his colour rose. He said:

"My wife has treated me abominably but I don't blame her as much as I do your Mr. Olver."

"I still find it so hard to believe that he could play such a dirty trick!" exclaimed Teresa.

"Are you very attached to him?"

"I'm not the sort to get attached to anybody—it's only one man for me. But I've enjoyed working for Mr. Olver because he's nice—or I thought so—and I admire his work. Still, after what you've told me I feel rather disgusted," she added.

"So it won't affect you very much if you see him fall from grace?"

"You mean the divorce and him being the co-respondent and all that?"

"More than that," said Guy softly.

Without understanding she continued to express her disappointment in Mr. Olver's character. Whatever she talked about, Guy noticed that she always turned back to the subject of the man she was living with and what she thought of him. The idiotic girl was infatuated with her unsuccessful film extra. Such was the power of sex, Guy reflected. He had felt that way about Toni once although not in the way she wanted and it was too bad that she hadn't liked *his* way. But it was established firmly in his mind now that Teresa Withers would do almost anything to keep in her young man's good books. To buy him all those new clothes he wanted, a car, and a lot of drinks, and then quit work and go abroad for a long holiday—if he'd like it. Oh, she was a great talker, Miss Withers, and nattered on about the things she'd like to do for Rod if only they weren't so hopelessly in debt. Guy already knew from the investigation that the pair were in debt to tradesmen all round them and late with their rent. Teresa was obviously the reliable one of the two but lost a lot of her reliability in the swamp of her desperate passion for her Rod.

Guy believed in making a sudden assault on the senses; it

invariably brought results. Suddenly he said:

"What would you say if I asked you to do something for me which you might not like doing but which would be of great service to me, and if I handed you *in cash* the sum, say, of ten thousand pounds?"

The coffee-spoon Teresa was holding clattered into the saucer. Her eyes goggled at Guy.

"Ten thousand pounds!" she repeated incredulously, "you have to be joking!"

"Far from it. I'm quite serious."

"But that's a fortune."

"I don't say that but it would help pay your bills and allow you to do all this entertaining and perhaps get your young man the work he wants. And of course you'd be very popular with him for doing so much for him, wouldn't you?"

Teresa swallowed several times—a hand up to her throat. She'd never been more surprised. *Shaken* was the word. It was the hell of a lot of money, that was certain. Ten years full salary—and for free, without working, and God knows she needed a rest. Looking after a well-known surgeon was pretty exhausting and the night life with Rod equally so. The money would be marvellous. Teresa pictured them meeting the right people and entertaining the film producers. It could have such *results. Ten thousand pounds in cash!*

Her heart palpitated—she didn't know whether it was indigestion after that big unaccustomed meal, or just sheer excitement. She rivetted her gaze on Mr. Brand, then into her confused mind came second thoughts; worried ones.

"Look here," she said, "what is it you'd want me to do in return for the money? It all sounds a bit like something dicey and something I oughtn't to do."

"Clever Teresa," he murmured, "you couldn't be more right."

"What is it then?"

Guy signalled to the waiter and ordered more coffee and two cognacs. He had by no means finished with Teresa.

12

"Tell me again—exactly what this tycoon wants you to do," said Rodney Best.

Teresa pouted.

"I've already told you twice."

"I want to hear it a third time, doll."

"Okay," she said.

Possibly Mr. Nathaniel Olver, F.R.C.S. would not have recognised his quiet homely staid secretary if he could have seen her that evening in her own environment. Teresa definitely had two faces to show—one for the world and one for her lover.

Tonight she wore not very clean bell-bottom trousers—vivid scarlet—with a lace shirt, and black satin bolero. Her coils of dark hair swung down her back. She had put on large dangling earrings and a chain belt. She looked gaudy, cheap and gypsy-like. A more voluptuous Teresa than the one who so quietly received Mr. Olver's patients. Even her voice changed to match Rodney's once she was with him. She tried to emulate his Americanisms. She liked being called 'a doll'. She thought it 'sexy'. She had had too many years of being the dull rather plain girl of the party, avoided by most of the men.

This room in the flatlet occupied by Teresa and Rod, with its kitchenette and none-too-savoury bathroom, was in its usual state of disorder. Rod chain-smoked and left his ash in every saucer and all over the blue-nylon carpet. There was nothing beautiful or artistic in the room except two quite fine gilt-framed prints of scenes in Portugal which had belonged to Teresa's family, and the silk-fringed shawl—her mother's—which was flung over one of the armchairs. The most expensive articles were the television and radiogram. Teresa had saved to buy them because Rod said they were essential to his work.

He lay this evening on the double divan, arms crossed behind his head and the inevitable cigarette hanging from his lower lip. Outside it was wet and cold but the little room was warm and stuffy. Rod had switched on an electric convector. It gave out a steady heat.

Teresa looked with adoration at the young man who had entered her life so suddenly eighteen months ago and absorbed it ever since. He was very slim—lithe hipped, like a matador—and as fair as Teresa was dark. She wasn't sure she really liked a man with long hair but she liked *his;* blond and silky, curling around his neck and shoulders. His complexion was pale; his high cheek-bones half hidden by a golden fuzz. He had narrow restless eyes and a greedy mouth. But he was handsome in his way and ever since he had known Teresa he had expressed an overwhelming need of her and given her abundant proof that she was the only girl with whom he had ever wanted to set up housekeeping. Of course she knew that he wasn't a good actor and that the most he could ever get was a one-line part or a walk-on, but he could be very entertaining at parties and gave amusing imitations of well-known stars. He played the guitar and sang—so Teresa thought—like an angel.

She fetched the instant coffee she had been making, poured out a mug for Rod and sipped hers while she repeated, obediently, her astonishing story.

This gentleman, tycoon as Rod called him, had offered her ten thousand pounds in cash to "cook the books" that Mr. Olver's secretary/receptionist had to keep, containing the names and appointments of his patients. The "cooking" meant that she, Teresa, must add the name of Mrs. Guy Brand to the list. One or two visits were enough but it was essential that Antonia Brand's name should be numbered amongst those women who had had consultations with Mr. Olver.

Teresa continued:

"Mr. Brand loathes Mr. Olver's guts because he has taken his, Mr. Brand's wife away. I'd say, after the talk I had with Mr. Brand, that he's absolutely obsessed with the desire to ruin my boss. The G.M.C. wouldn't do anything if it's a straight divorce, but perhaps caution Mr. Olver, and he might get the occasional cold shoulder at his hospital. But he could still practise. Mr. Brand wants to fix it so he *can't*. You can see for yourself that if the G.M.C. believe that he's committed adultery with a patient, he's had it."

Rodney considered this for a moment, then took the cigarette from his lips and burst out laughing.

"What a set-up! Doesn't sound realistic to me. Are you sure you haven't been reading too many paper-backs?"

"Don't be silly, honey, of course it's true or I wouldn't have told you."

"And let's hear again what *you* told Mr. Brand."

"Well, at first I was pretty shocked. I really was, Rod. I'm no angel. I'd do lots of wrong things like living with you when we're not married, smoking 'pot' and all that, but being the instrument of ruining a nice man like my boss, is quite another thing."

"Cut out the heroics, baby. Let's have it straight. You turned down the offer?"

"Yes. At least I said I'd think it over."

"Glad you added that."

Teresa pushed back her strand of heavy black hair and gaped at Rod.

"You aren't suggesting that I—"

"I'm suggesting that you *do* think it over," he cut in.

She got up, found a cigarette, lit it and began to walk up and down the room.

"I just couldn't, Rod. It's tempting but I would have to be

really unscrupulous to do such a thing."

His gaze followed the plump figure in the red satin and white lace. He liked Teresa best when she was dressed like this. She looked dishy, and with that long black hair tumbling down her back, quite desirable. She hadn't a bad figure even though she was on the big size, very good legs, too, and as a sex-companion she was pretty good. Apart from that she was unfailingly generous to him.

Rod had few principles. He had come up from the gutter, he was still a guttersnipe in the recess of his being, although he could ape the elegant educated actor if he wished. Or the amusing entertainer, strumming on his guitar, crooning folk-songs. He knew perfectly well that there were many much more attractive and prettier girls than Teresa both in the theatre, film-studios, and T.V. but they did not all earn good steady money like his clever Teresa. For many long months now Rod had been out of work and unable to keep himself. Teresa was his anchor in a sea of trouble. He was genuinely fond of her in his way. She was mother, sister, wife and slave. He enjoyed it. But *this*—this new project was both staggering and exciting. He gave a little whistle which made her turn round and come to the bedside. He held out a hand and drew her down.

"Listen, doll, you and I could have one hell of a good time on ten thousand pounds."

"I don't doubt it," said Teresa, her face flushed and her lashes flickering nervously. The whole business made her feel nervous and ill-at-ease, "but I just can't do it, Rod."

"You're going to turn down ten thousand pounds cash just for the sake of a few principles?"

"More than that, Rod—I'd be breaking the law. It would make me a sort of criminal if I did it. I'd risk being sent to gaol."

"Rubbish. It would only be your doctor's word against yours. They'd say the wife was lying to save *him*. Nobody could prove you'd deliberately cooked the books, could they? Nobody but you know what women come in and out of Olver's consulting room."

"There's a man in the main hall who lets people in but he wouldn't remember and certainly wouldn't be able to swear he had never seen Mrs. Brand."

Rod pulled Teresa down and gave her one of the kisses that had become as necessary to her hungry body as her daily bread.

"Then, my dear little Teresa, you wouldn't be incriminated. Okay?"

"Maybe not but I—I wouldn't know how to face Mr. Olver if I testified against him. My God, he's a nice guy, Rod, and innocent. And he's always trusted me."

Rod flung out his arms and rolled his eyes.

"You slay me, honey. You're so full of piety today. You're too good for me. Why don't you quit this den of vice and enter a convent? You'd make a nice cosy nun."

"Don't be beastly," she flashed, "and really, Rod, I thought *you* had a few principles."

"Absolutely none, dearest," he said with a wide smile and that melting look in his eyes that never failed to stir her blood. She felt her body trembling with desire for him. She knew that his talk about her quitting and becoming a nun had been a joke. But the mere idea of losing him and all the excitement, passion and pleasure that she enjoyed in her life with him horrified her.

He ran his fore-finger across her thick dark brows, then her moist lips.

"You're really rather gorgeous," he said dreamily.

Suddenly she hung on to him.

"I could never leave you, never. You know that."

"And I don't ever want to lose you, baby. We hit it off very well."

Teresa covered his face with kisses. She was too deeply

involved with her own feelings and her existence with this boy to go on being too squeamish and analytical of the situation. She glossed over the thought that she was always the "giver" in this set-up and he, the "taker". She didn't care. Yet to bear false witness against an innocent man and have him thrown out of the medical profession in consequence would be not only breaking the law and one of the Commandments, but hitting below the belt in a big way.

"Oh, Rod," she said in a muffled voice, "I didn't ought to do it."

"Okay, there are lots of things we didn't ought to do, love. Let this be one."

She raised her head and looked at him, breathing heavily.

"You can't mean that you *want* me to take the offer!"

He pushed her gently away, spread out both hands and shrugged his shoulders.

"Honey-chile," he said with a Southern drawl, "have you really imagined what it would be like to get that ten thousand pounds? Crisp bank notes, *cash*, without working for it, and all for us to spend?"

"Of course I can imagine it, but I just would sooner not get rich that way. Oh, I admit I'd like the money as much as you would. I'd like it more than anything for *you*."

"And I'd like it for you," he lied gullibly. "You've spent so much on me, I'd get a kick out of seeing my little Teresa with enough money in her purse to go and buy all the things she wants. We'd be careful of say half the lolly and invest it and enjoy the rest. We'd nip down to the South of France and try our luck at the Casino. And I'd get hold of the film contacts I need. I'd give a supper party and ask all the guys who could help feather my nest. *And*—listen, doll—" Rod continued to pour out a further list of the things he could do, and that they could buy if they had that ten thousand pounds.

What he didn't suggest aloud (because he did not want to shock Teresa too greatly) was a sudden idea that the tycoon might perhaps be touched in the future for a few more of those bank notes. Just a *very* little blackmail. Why, the whole set-up had endless possibilities. It intrigued Rod. As for helping to ruin the doctor—what did it matter to them? He'd been a fool and Rod saw no reason to pity fools. Olver was in a good profession and earned good money; why risk losing it all, as he'd done, for the sake of a doll? Teresa said Mrs. Brand was supposed to be a raving beauty. *But I,* thought Rod, *wouldn't fling away my chances for any female—not if she was Miss World herself.*

Teresa started to weaken.

"I really couldn't bring myself to do this thing," she kept mumbling.

Rod tried other tactics. He pulled her down to him and ran his fingers through her long dark hair. He looked at her with the passion he could so easily summon up when it was to get his own way.

"Not even for me? Wouldn't you even do it for me, Teresa baby? I've never had so much money in my whole life. Neither have you. We can't turn that offer down just out of Christian charity. Mind you, I think your tycoon's round the bend, and the girl must be quite something to get her husband into such a state because she's left him. But why worry ourselves about crazy people? And if what you say is true, he's a millionaire, so what's ten thou to him? Let him give it to us and in return you do what's needed. Only be quite certain you don't put Mrs. B.'s name in that appointment book till you've made sure of the cash. You'll have to be clever and make it look as though the appointments were on various dates before she went away with the doctor."

Teresa was silent. She still had a glimmer of conscience about this thing. She couldn't view the affair with quite Rod's total lack of concern. But she didn't despise him for it. She only knew that if she did as Mr. Brand asked and brought all that money back to Rod, she'd dole it out and never lose him.

It would be a tie he would never break.

He went on kissing and caressing her. She burst into tears and he let her cry. Rod was not without knowledge of feminine psychology and he knew his Teresa and her weaknesses. It wasn't long before he had her where he wanted her—completely subjugated.

"Oh, I love you, I'm mad about you," she cried hysterically, "I'll do anything to make you really happy."

He whispered against her ear.

"I haven't a single trouble in the world, sweetie, that ten thousand pounds can't take care of. Now dry your eyes and we'll nip over to the pub for our drinks. It may be vodka and lime tonight, but by the time you've finished playing your part in this little drama, it'll be caviar and champagne."

"Okay, I'll do what Mr. Brand asks," said Teresa, and with those words went right down into the dark swirling waters of madness—the madness of her passion for Rod which persuaded her to commit a crime in order to destroy Nathaniel Olver.

In the end she felt ready to risk anything—even if it meant becoming an accessory after the fact. She knew that never again could she bear to live alone and be the odd girl out at the party if she was ever asked to one. Rod and Rod's wishes must come first.

*   *   *

She tried to close her mind to her guilt when she faced her employer that next morning. It was routine work—taking down letters before the first patient arrived.

"You work very hard, Teresa. I don't know what I'd do without you. You're a genius for getting all the medical terms spelled correctly and being tactful with my patients. I do appreciate it, you know. But I don't want to overwork you."

Teresa bent low over her stenographer's pad. A dull red had crept up under her sallow skin. But she shut both eyes and ears to her conscience. She'd had a wonderful night with Rod last night. He'd never been more amorous, or made life more glamorous for her. It was wonderful what the thought of all that money could do; and, after all, Guy Brand had some right to be revengeful. Mr. Olver had taken his wife away, hadn't he? He deserved what was coming.

"I'm fine, thanks, Mr. Olver," she said in answer to his sympathetic comments, and retired to her own room to transcribe her notes.

*　　　*　　　*

That night, Nat took Toni out to dinner; to a small Italian restaurant they had patronised before, because it was quiet. They had never yet met anybody they knew there.

"You're looking better, darling," he said as she sat down opposite him. "Did you have a good night?"

"Yes, I slept better, thank you, darling."

"Anything of interest to tell me?"

"Nothing. Chris advised me to get my own lawyer on the job—obviously I can't go to Guy's—so I had a word with Joe's man, a Mr. Johnson of Johnson and Hicks in Lincoln's Inn. He was very helpful and said of course I must be represented if I didn't intend to defend the divorce when it came up, and that it was absolutely in order for me to send for my own belongings from the penthouse. I shan't of course touch any of the clothes or furs or valuables that Guy bought me. But if he won't give me my own things I can get a court order."

"So you shall."

"I can manage with the things you've given me and I don't any longer have to be the sort of fashion model I was forced to be with Guy."

Nat smiled at her.

"Well, I hope you won't have to go into purdah entirely once you're my wife, my love."

123

"I don't mind as long as I stay No. 1 harem-favourite," she said. And now she was laughing and he was delighted to find her in so much better form.

He had nothing special to tell her about himself. Guy had not yet had time to spread his poison through the hospital via Lord Sydell, nor to get his solicitors to issue a formal petition for the divorce. That pleasure was to come, said Nat drily. But he had reached one conclusion—he intended to leave his present flat—hand it over completely to Mervyn if he wanted it —and rent a temporary place which he could share with Toni, and where they could live as man and wife. It wasn't much good their plunging into all this trouble and anxiety if they were to remain apart. At least they should have the consolation of living together. It was expected of them.

"I couldn't agree more," said Toni, and looking quickly round the crowded little restaurant, she added in a low voice, "I absolutely loathe being away from you."

13

They spent the rest of that evening in the Masters' maisonette. Joe and Chris were out for dinner. Chris had suggested that Toni should benefit by their absence. They had three wonderful hours together. Toni felt a great deal less harassed about the whole situation before Nat left, later that night. He, himself, seemed calm and relaxed.

"We've got a lot to look forward to now, darling," he said. "It's all been a bit of a shock—up till now we've both been stunned, but let's make the most of the moments we can be together. Personally I'm fully prepared for whatever happens in the future and I'm going to make damned sure nothing too frightful upsets *you*."

She kissed him with passion and gratitude.

"I'm just not used to someone worrying about me all the time the way you do. It's terrific."

"I adore you, Toni," he said, "I'll never stop being glad things have turned out this way."

She said softly:

"We certainly never thought when we first went off the deep end that we were going to drown, but it's glorious drowning with you, my darling Nat."

They parted on a wave of optimism. One week later the most stunning blow of all descended on them and destroyed what little peace or happiness they had regained.

*   *   *

During that week Nat had been so busy that he had found

no time to search for a home he could share with Toni, and she, having begun work at Bertrand's, was equally busy. But she was enjoying her job. She had no feelings of embarrassment or irritation because she, wearing a pale pink overall, was now just 'a girl who shampooed hair' instead of being a favoured client. It even amused her. And when she took home her first pay packet on Friday night, she waved it triumphantly at Chris.

"Look at this! I can pay for my board and lodging with you and that means a lot to me."

"Now really, I refuse to take a penny—" began Chris but was talked down by Toni.

"Till Nat and I set up together, I pay my way!"

The doorbell rang. Chris answered it. She returned to the sitting room where Toni was relaxing, her tired feet curled up under her and her pay packet on her lap.

"It's your boy-friend."

"Nat?" asked Toni in surprise, "I thought he was going to some sort of hospital-do tonight."

"Well, he isn't, and he seems in a state and wants to see you urgently. He's just putting his car on a meter now. He didn't know whether you were in or out till he saw me. When he comes back I'll disappear. I've got some ironing to do before Joe gets home."

Toni was in good spirits as she put on her shoes and stood up to meet Nat as he walked into the room. The October night was stormy and cold, but she felt warm. An electric fire was burning, sending out a rosy glow. But the gay greeting Toni had prepared for Nat and any idea of flaunting her pay-packet at him, vanished as she saw his face. He was ashen. She exclaimed:

"*Nat!* What on earth's the matter? You look ghastly!"

"I'm afraid what I've got to tell you *is* pretty ghastly," he said.

"Oh, my God, what's happened now?"

"Something quite *quite* fantastically unbelievable."

She grew suddenly cold.

"Nat, you frighten me."

He handed her a letter which he took from a long legal-looking envelope.

"You'd better read this."

*   *   *

Toni, her heart sinking, examined the letter. She had at once recognised the notepaper and its heading. She had seen it so often during her life with Guy. It was from his solicitors, and addressed to Mr. Nathaniel Olver, F.R.C.S.

"Dear Sir,

Our client, Mr. Guy Brand, wishes to inform you that unless his wife returns to him within the next ten days he intends to petition for divorce and cite you as co-respondent for which he has full evidence. He wishes you also to know that he has now received further proof that Mrs. Brand was a patient of yours and his receptionist, Miss Teresa Withers, is willing to testify to this fact. She has produced the necessary documents of ratification.

We would like to point out that in giving Mrs. Brand the opportunity to return to him, Mr. Brand is showing great generosity. At the same time he wishes us to point out to you that if the divorce is to proceed you will now come under the jurisdiction of the General Medical Council.

> *Yours truly . . ."*

There followed the signature of the senior partner who was Guy's special friend.

Toni lifted her head and gasped.

"But this is absolutely outrageous! He can't *do* this. I never have been your patient. What does it mean that your receptionist is willing to testify that I am? Is she out of her mind?"

Nat, who was standing with his back to the fire, his lean

angular body shaking a little, gave a curt laugh.

"Well, if she isn't, we are—right out of our tiny minds! I tell you, Toni, that this letter came as an absolute bombshell. I only got it just before I left my room for home. I phoned through to the hospital to say I had developed a temperature and couldn't go out. I *couldn't* sit through a formal dinner with this document burning a hole in my pocket. I had to come and discuss it with you."

She walked to him, and put both arms around his waist, hugging him against her.

"Oh, my darling, I'm so glad you have come, but *what does it mean*? Have you tackled Miss What's-her-name, Teresa Something-or-other?"

"No, she'd gone home early. I was making one or two phone calls, then going back to change for the hospital dinner. But I did phone the solicitors. Mr. Johnson had already left so I spoke to this Mr. Johnson's head clerk. He knew all about it. I gave him a firm denial of the fact that you were ever one of my patients. He then confounded me by saying they had that very morning seen the book in which your name was entered as having had two consultations. They also produced a receipt —at least a carbon copy of one—for fees paid in cash by you, and stamped with my official stamp. No evidence could be more plain or damning."

"But it isn't true. I've never consulted you," said Toni stupidly. She felt stupid. Her temples throbbed. Her knees were trembling.

"Of course I intend to see Teresa at once," said Nat. "I know where she lives. She must have some explanation."

Toni broke out wildly:

"She's been bribed to do this. It's obvious. I warned you that Guy's a fiend. I bet you a thousand pounds he's bribed her to tell this lie and I suppose she *could* even forge a receipt."

"Guy may be a fiend but he can't be so mad as that. It's a criminal act. He could ruin himself instead of me. For of course we'll have to defend the case now. I'll get the best counsel and no matter what it costs me, I'll prove that this new evidence has been trumped up."

Toni looked at him with a face of blank despair. It was the most awful thing that had ever happened, she thought: so awful that it froze her. She could neither think nor speak.

Nat noticed her expression, quickly put his arms around her and kissed her on both cheeks.

"Don't look like that, darling. I can't bear it. And don't despair. You don't suppose I'll sit under this nonsense, do you?"

She shook her head and pressed her face against his shoulder.

In a queer way she felt that Nat's kisses on her cheeks rather than her lips—seemed symbolic of what was to come. No passion no matter how great could stand up to this sort of beating, and with Guy wielding such an unholy whip she could imagine that for the moment anyhow Nat in his masculine way had little desire for loving. *This* was outside all his suppositions of what might happen to him. From the very beginning he had been sure that featuring in a divorce would not give the G.M.C. the slightest chance to throw him out of the profession.

I've done this, she thought, *I let him take me away. They say the woman's always got it in her power to say yes or no. I said yes and it's going to ruin him.*

He put her gently away from him and lit a cigarette.

"Do you think Joe would mind if you pinch a drink for me. I need one. Then I shall drive round to Teresa's flat."

"Of course," Toni said, pulling herself together, "I'll pour you out a whisky. Joe wouldn't mind a bit, and anyhow Chris is in the kitchen. I can let her know later. Let me come to this flat with you, please."

"I'd rather you didn't."

"Very well," she said dully.

He drank the whisky she brought, then put on his coat.

She walked with him to the front door. He turned and said:

"Keep quiet about this for the moment, darling. I haven't had time to sort things out. I must see Teresa first."

She nodded.

"You'll come back here?"

"Yes, darling."

Then he was gone.

*   *   *

Toni told Chris that Nat had to go out for a moment, then sat down by the fire again, alone, trying to get warm. The shock of what he had just told her had frozen her body as well as her mind. She sat there, shivering, thinking, *thinking*, firm in her belief that this hideous plot was of Guy's engineering. How he had done it, or why Nat's trusted secretary had stooped to co-operate with him in such a dastardly act, she did not know.

Her mind almost seemed to stop working during the hour Nat was away. When he did come back, she saw at once that things had not improved. His face was grey. All warmth and love seemed to have been wiped from it. But he took her cold hands, kissed them and spoke to her with customary gentleness.

"You look rotten, my poor love. Come and sit down again and we'll talk."

"Did you see Teresa?"

"No. Only her boy-friend. This Rodney something she lives with. He didn't ask me in. He just spoke to me at the door."

"What did he say?"

"That Teresa is ill in bed—conveniently ill, I imagine, and wouldn't be coming back to work for me anyhow, and would I please just send the salary due to her up to date."

"Oh, God," whispered Toni.

Nat was sitting in an armchair, his long fingers locked about his knees, his eyes staring into the pink glow of the fire.

He began to tell her about the conversation he had had with Rodney.

He described his secretary's boy-friend as an unappetising hippie-type, and the glimpse Nat had of the hall had nauseated him. It looked as though it had not been cleaned for ages—like the young man, Nat added. It seemed extraordinary to him that Teresa who was so scrupulous in her appearance when she was at work, should lead such a life privately. He asked her boy-friend—Rodney Best was his name, Nat remembered now—if he knew what was going on, and Best admitted that he did. In fact he leered at Nat in a way that made the older man wish he could knock him down. Then Best made some crack about "Naughty—naughty Doc living it up with a patient". Nat kept his temper and asked if Mr. Best would kindly enlighten him about this testimony Teresa was to give. Teresa, he told Best, knew perfectly well that Mrs. Brand had never been a patient of his. Was it true that Teresa intended to swear that she had?

Rodney Best then said that Teresa was fully justified in this because she had often told *him* that Mr. Olver was "knocking around with one of his patients".

"I remarked at the time that Mr. Olver would get himself into trouble if he did that sort of thing," Best had said, a hateful grin on his lips, and added that naturally when Mr. Brand asked Teresa if his wife had ever consulted Mr. Olver, she had to speak the truth. It was in the book, and there were two receipts for the cash Mrs. Brand had given Teresa for her consultations before she left.

Now Nat raised his face to Toni. His eyes were red-rimmed with exhaustion.

"I did lose my temper then, I admit it. I shouted and I hope Teresa heard me. I told them that it was all a pack of bloody awful lies and the whole job had been manoeuvred by Guy Brand and that I'd defend the case and spend my last penny if necessary to prove that you were *not* my patient and never had been."

Toni put the tips of her fingers to her lips. Her eyes looked enormous.

"God in heaven!" she said. "How could anybody be so vile? Of course Guy bribed Teresa. I have no doubt about it now. And she's doing it for the boy-friend. It's obvious."

"And the court shall be made to see it," muttered Nat. "I've got a very good friend—one of the best Counsels in London. He specialises in divorce cases. He'll fight this for us."

Toni uttered a sound which was half a sob, half an hysterical laugh.

"It's worse than a nightmare. Quite fantastic. It's something we never anticipated. Even though I knew Guy was vindictive, I didn't think he'd stoop to this. Of course I know we're only guessing that he bribed your secretary, but there can't be any other explanation. It's his ghastly jealousy—he's so furious he lost me!"

"Quite so," said Nat grimly.

Toni knelt down beside him, encircled him with her arms and laid her cheek against his knee.

"Nat, Nat, what are we going to do? Do you really think your Counsel friend could win? Or have Guy and this ghastly girl between them been so cunning that it'll only be a question of our word against their faked evidence?"

He put a hand on her hair and stroked it automatically.

"I don't know," he said slowly, "we'll just have to see. I must admit it's knocked me for six. Actually I can't think very straight tonight, but I'm not going to let Guy get away with this or hurt you any more. I swear before God I won't."

"*He'll* have a good Counsel too," she whispered.

"Oh, yes. The next thing he'll do is to send the necessary papers to some big wig or other in order to settle the petition."

Toni thought:

It won't be a fair fight with Guy behind it. He used to

132

boast that he's never lost a legal action yet.

And what made it all the more ironic was the fact that obviously Teresa Withers, who was proving such a snake in the grass, needed money for her boy-friend. It was her passion for him that had done this. Money would pass between her and Guy in such a manner that it couldn't be traced.

Suddenly Nat got up and pulled her on to her feet.

"Will you forgive me, darling, if I go home? I can't stand any more tonight. I had rather a long day operating and then this coming on top of it. I've got an extremely important operation first thing in the morning, too. I must try to get some sleep somehow."

"But you haven't had any dinner—" she began.

"I don't want any. And forgive me, darling, if I don't take you out."

"You know that doesn't matter. I couldn't eat a thing."

Nat pulled her into his arms.

"Well, it's no use our going to pieces," he said with a short laugh. "The great thing is that we love each other and we're not going to allow Mr. Brand's craze for revenge to come between *us*."

Toni's heart leapt at those words but she stayed silent.

"Don't mention this to Chris for the moment," Nat added before he left and told her that he would see her tomorrow as soon as he got through his various commitments.

Woman-like, Toni would have liked to have stayed with him tonight; to comfort him and be comforted. But she could see that his wish was to be alone in order to think the whole thing out.

Already, she thought, *Guy has managed to put a spoke between us.*

She, herself, began to feel that the situation was changing. She had been willing to accept Nat's sacrifice if it had only meant him standing as an ordinary co-respondent in an ordinary divorce case. But tonight she went back on all previous decisions. She knew that she would never allow *this* divorce to take place. Not if there was a chance that Guy might get away with his criminal plan to finish Nat's career.

She pleaded a sick headache and excused herself from having supper with Chris and Joe. Chris accepted the excuse. She was, in fact, too busy with her baby who was being fractious tonight and with her other domestic chores, to pay much attention to Toni. Alone in her own room, Toni walked up and down, up and down, sorting things out in her mind.

Supposing the case came up and Guy won it and the G.M.C. struck Nat off for misconducting himself with a patient? He would have to find other work, give up his beloved career as a gynaecologist—find a job perhaps in a small laboratory, or some concern where they didn't care about his reputation—or even work abroad, since he could no longer practise in this country.

It would mean a hole-in-the-corner life for him. *She* wouldn't mind being poor, or ostracised—even if all his savings went in defence of his honour. She would be happy with him anywhere in the world and under any circumstances. But he was a man and a surgeon. *How would he feel about her in time?*

She was neither so romantic or so stupid as to suppose that even the greatest passion could stand up to this sort of revolution in a man's life. Nat might still love her but he would never in his heart cease to regret the status he had lost. He would feel even more deeply as time went on the appalling injustice of having been so wronged. With all the love and care in the world, she wouldn't be able to make up to him for that.

It was now that Toni remembered what Guy had once said over the telephone: *"You won't be happy . . . he won't thank you. . . . When his work goes down and even ceases altogether, he'll end up by wishing that he had never met you."*

The significance of those words hit her with full force this evening. Nat was a fine man and a tender lover—but he was only human. He *might* in time go the way Guy prophesied—*might grow to hate her*.

Suddenly Toni rushed into the bathroom and was violently sick.

She went back to her room and sat on the bed, shivering. She felt calmer. Calm enough to be able to look at things sanely and to foresee some of the eventualities in the future with Nat —if there was to be a future! And *if* she allowed the divorce to take place.

The idea of leaving him and never seeing him again and of going back to Guy was so hideous that she could not swallow it just in a moment—just in an hour—just in a night.

Something might happen tomorrow to end this nightmare. Teresa might have a change of heart—perhaps.

I'll go and see Teresa myself. The idea leapt into Toni's mind.

How would she get the address? Not from Nat. He wouldn't want her to go near his ex-receptionist or be involved. But once having decided that it might do some good if she could talk to Teresa, the idea refused to leave Toni's tormented mind.

Nat and the other doctor—Lucas-Wright—would have to get a temporary replacement for their receptionist. They couldn't manage without one. She would wait until she knew it was Nat's time to be at the hospital, then she would telephone his consulting room.

With the aid of a sleeping pill Toni managed to get a few hours sleep that night. She also managed to avoid any questioning from Chris. She made up her face, put plenty of colour on her cheeks and was deliberately gay during breakfast with the family in the kitchen. It was important that she should retain her job—for the moment, anyhow—until the situation was clarified but she could not have stood hairdressing today, and listening to clients' chatter. She rang up the shop, pleaded a feverish cold and promised to be in the next day.

* * *

135

She waited until Chris was out of the house, shopping, then dialled the number of Nat's consulting room. There was no reply. An hour before lunch she went out to a call box and dialled the number again. This time a woman answered. A replacement had been found.

"Could I speak to Miss Withers?" asked Toni.

"Miss Withers is not here. She's been taken ill, I'm afraid, I'm a friend of Mr. Lucas-Wright. I am making appointments for him and for Mr. Olver, temporarily. They expect to have a new receptionist tomorrow."

Toni told her that she was a personal friend of Miss Withers, and could she please have her home-address which Toni had lost. The woman asked her to hold on. She would see if she could find it in the address book, either on Mr. Lucas-Wright's or Mr. Olver's desks. Both the doctors were out.

To Toni's relief the address was found and given to her. Toni took a taxi straight there. Teresa's home was in a gloomy out-dated block of mansion flats in a cul-de-sac off Baker Street.

Some of Toni's courage ebbed as she rang the bell. Nat would be furious with her for doing this. Perhaps she ought to run away before it was too late. What was she letting herself in for? But it *was* too late. The front door opened. She saw a girl wearing slacks and a pullover and with a cigarette hanging from her lower lip, standing in the hall.

She knew at once that this was Teresa Withers. Nat had described her. The black hair piled up on her head, the greasy skin, the full figure. She felt a complete loathing for this girl who was willing to help wreck Nat's career, yet a touch of pity. It must be awful to be so infatuated with a man that one could stoop to criminal action for his sake. Nat some time ago had mentioned the fact that Teresa was keeping an out-of-work film extra. They needed money—Guy had undoubtedly offered them plenty to lie on his behalf.

Teresa stared without recognition at the attractive-looking girl with the big golden eyes. But her expression changed once Toni bluntly introduced herself.

"You're Miss Withers, aren't you? I'm Mrs. Guy Brand. May I come in? I want a word with you."

Teresa gave a gasp. The penny had dropped. She knew now who her caller was. She tried to close the front door, but Toni was fighting for Nat and it gave her unusual strength and determination. She pushed her way into the flat, her lips pressed together.

"You can't come into my place like this—" began Teresa.

"But I'm here," said Toni calmly, "and I mean to speak to you so you might as well ask me to sit down."

Teresa's face was scarlet. She felt definitely nervous. It was a damned nuisance that Rod had had a call to the studios this morning, for 'a walk-on' in a crowd scene.

"Well, I think this is cheek—" she began sullenly.

"And I think what you are trying to do to Mr. Olver is absolutely abominable," cut in Toni and marched into the studio.

It was as disordered as ever. Toni looked around her with disgust—ash all over the floor; double divan bed still unmade and rumpled; a pile of lurid-looking paper-backs on a table, with two empty beer bottles and dirty glasses. It mystified Toni that the receptionist-secretary whom Nat had described as so neat and clean and efficient should be like this in her own home. Obviously the boy-friend was a bad influence and Teresa too infatuated to see the wood for the trees.

Neither of the girls sat down. They faced each other defiantly. Toni came straight to the point.

"Miss Withers, you sent false testimony to my—my husband's solicitors, and you intend to back it up in the courts if questioned. You know as well as I do, don't you, that I have never so much as entered Mr. Olver's consulting room and that I have *never* been a patient of his."

Teresa licked her lips. She was shaken by Mrs. Brand's

personal appearance. *My*, she thought, *she's a beauty and no mistake, but I'm not going to have her coming the haughty lady with me. Neither am I going to feel all that much conscience-stricken. As Rod said, she's done wrong and so has Mr. Olver.*

Teresa made up her mind then and there to take a stand and behave as though this dirty trick she and Rod were playing was no fabrication.

"I just don't know why you've come here to say such things, Mrs. Brand. You know perfectly well you came to consult Mr. Olver on two occasions. *And* you paid in cash—you said you'd rather not send a cheque, and of course, now I know why. You didn't want your husband to see it in your bank book."

Toni curled her lips.

"You're wrong there. I've never owned a cheque book. My husband pays all my bills."

"All the more reason why you didn't want *him* to have to pay and see that you had to consult a gynaecologist."

Toni flushed.

"I'm not sure what you're implying, but the fact remains that I did not consult Mr. Olver and that you are saying that I did because you've been bribed by my husband to do so."

Teresa gulped. She was a little surprised that Mrs. Brand had cottoned on to the truth so easily.

"That's a B-Y awful thing to say!" She spoke in a loud voice—"Suggesting that I'm willing to commit perjury for money."

"Well, aren't you?" asked Toni. "Don't forget that I know my husband. He'd go to any lengths to punish the man who has taken me from him."

"I don't know what you're talking about and I must ask you to leave my flat. I'm not prepared to listen to your insults."

Now some of Toni's courage evaporated. She saw that she was going to get no change out of Miss Withers and she was utterly dismayed by the thought of the harm Teresa could do

138

if she carried out her infamous intention.

Toni tried another tone.

"Miss Withers," she said in a low voice, "I beg you to reconsider this thing. You do know that it *isn't* true. It doesn't really matter why you have agreed to commit perjury although I take it for granted my husband is at the back of it. But I *beg you* not to go through with it. Not for my sake—for Mr. Olver's. I'm just as—f—fond of him as you must be of the young man you're living with. You'd do anything for him, I can see that, and I'd do anything for Mr. Olver. We're two women in love—surely we can understand each other. Surely you can see how terrible this will be for me. Even though I'm only partially responsible, I assure you I'd never have gone away with Mr. Olver if I had been his patient. I was well aware that would have meant ruin for him. Please, please, Miss Withers, don't do this. How could you live with yourself if you did? He's never done you any harm, has he?"

Silence from Teresa. She stared not at Toni but at the floor. Steeped in guilt, in the crazy wish to get the money for Rod— she was still ashamed of herself at the bottom of it all. But it was too late to draw back now. When she had handed Mr. Brand the forged carbon receipt for the consultation fee—made out to Mrs. Brand—he had given her the first payment. Two hundred and fifty pounds in bank-notes. She and Rod had got 'stinking' on the strength of it. He wouln't have gone to the studio to play that small part if he hadn't wanted to say goodbye to them all. He'd boast that he'd 'come into money'. He and Teresa were going to nip over to Monte Carlo by air, tomorrow. They'd be back long before the divorce. Then Teresa could play her part. It was agreed that Mr. Brand would pay the remaining bulk of the money into some bank abroad for them. He had so many business contacts, it meant nothing to him. He could arrange for it in Geneva.

Rod was delirious, half-crazy with excitement. She was never out of his arms. She had never been more thrilled. She wasn't going to let conscience queer the pitch now. She knew perfectly well that if she did, Rod would leave her.

"Miss Withers," Toni repeated the name pleadingly, "please, I beg you, don't do this thing to Mr. Olver. He's one of the best men in the world and a dedicated doctor."

All that was bad in Teresa rose to the surface. She sneered: "B-Y good—going off for a holiday with another man's wife."

Toni, crimson, fully alive to what *she* had done, stammered: "All right. Say anything you like to me, or about me. But don't lie about him. Don't say he was *my* doctor."

"I've done it and shall repeat it in court," said Teresa in a loud blustering voice, "And now please get out, I've got work to do."

Toni was beaten. She knew it. It was obvious that Teresa Withers was quite unscrupulous and unrepentant.

Oh God, Toni thought despairingly, *the awful power of money. I've always known it. Living with Guy taught me that. It's vile—vile!*

Then she was in the hall and the front door slammed behind her.

* * *

She stumbled down the stone staircase and out into the street. In contrast with recent weather it was a beautiful crisp autumn morning with a clear blue sky. Toni looked around with frightened eyes. She'd gone to see Nat's Receptionist hoping against hope to put an end to the threats that were sinking him, and she had failed.

Her first thought was to hail a taxi but she curbed that extravagance and went back to Brompton Road by bus.

She found Chris in the kitchen coping with the usual pile of ironing—Joe's shirts and some things of the baby's.

Chris put down her iron as she saw her friend's face. She knew Toni well. She hardly recognised her; she was deathly white and there was a look in her eyes that frightened Chris.

"Darling!" she exclaimed and came forward and took the bag from Toni's hand. She made her sit down, "What on *earth* has happened now?"

"I'll tell you," said Toni in a dull voice. "It all started when Nat came to see me last night and told me what had happened. Now I can tell you because I've absolutely decided to go back to Guy and nothing, *nobody*, will make me change my mind."

14

That night when Nat called at the little maisonette in Ovington Gardens, Joe Masters met him in the hall.

Nat rather liked Joe. He was a solid dependable, pleasant sort of young man and obviously devoted to his family. The sort Nat was fast beginning to wish he had been himself. Joe in a similar position to his, out of the public eye, quite unknown, in fact, would never have been plunged into this kind of chaos nor caused the woman he loved so much trouble.

As a rule Nat didn't see Joe when he called here. Joe kept out of Nat's way, but tonight he had an uncomfortable duty to perform and he agreed to do it. Chris was too tender-hearted—so she had told her husband earlier on—she would only break down and weep if she started, so it would be better for Joe to deal with the unfortunate Nat.

Just how unfortunate, Nat did not realise until he was standing by the electric fire where he had sat last night with Toni, and his world had seemed to be crashing around him. He took the letter that Joe handed him. Before opening it, he asked:

"Is Toni in?"

"No, and I'm afraid she won't be living here any more."

"Won't be?" Nat echoed, brows knit. "What do you mean? Has she gone to live somewhere else?"

"Look," Joe said, "let me give you a whisky or something and you sit here quietly, have a drink and read your letter."

Mystified, and somewhat alarmed, Nat sat down. He read what Toni had written before he touched the drink so kindly given him by Joe.

He was glad he had been left alone. The shock of Toni's letter was so great he would have found it difficult to speak even to Toni's great friends. He read the letter again and again until he had absorbed every word and the full significance of it battered its way into his consciousness.

"Nat, my darling, darling Nat, I don't suppose you'll ever forgive me for this but in time perhaps you'll be grateful.

I've just had lunch with Chris. I've talked things over with her. She doesn't altogether agree with what I mean to do, but she admits that in the face of this awful new development in our affairs, the whole question of a divorce has changed.

I went to see Teresa Withers this morning. I tried to make her realise what a crime she is committing, and to refute her statement. I also said that we meant to defend the case but that hardly shook her. She's got Guy and Guy's money behind her of course. She and her boy-friend feel pretty secure. Any-how, although she refused to discuss it, or admit that Guy is behind it, she is determined to go through with her lies. In fact she behaved as though it was true that I'd been your patient and that she had every right to say so. I suppose she engineered that book of records so that it looks genuine and the carbon copy of the receipt made out to me was a stroke of genius.

So, my darling Nat, I cannot go through with this. I'd rather live with Guy for the rest of my life. He's given me the chance to go back and I must accept it. It means now that he is condoning our affair and won't file his petition. Neither will he ever mention your name to Lord Sydell so your reputation will be quite safe.

Nat, I know that you'll be furious with me and I'm sure that you love me enough to want to carry on, and I also imagine you'll be deeply hurt. You'll hate to think of me back with Guy. On the other hand I was prepared to accept my life with him until I met you and we fell in love, so I can take it *again*, and believe me, *I've* struck a bargain with Guy. *I've* told him if he doesn't stop bullying and tormenting me *I'll* leave him at a future date when all this has died down and that next time it won't be for another man. *I'll* just live alone.

I know you intended to defend the case, but even if you won it plus damages, it would still be bad publicity for you. Your name would be in all the papers. Just think of the Sunday press. It would be grim. Anyhow I don't see how it can possibly be proved that I didn't consult you if that awful girl swears I did and produces the evidence. So I refuse to let you be struck off by the G.M.C. I told you right from the start that I would never do that, didn't I?

Oh, my darling, no matter how wonderful you might be to me in the future or what sort of existence we managed to build up, I would always feel responsible for having disgraced you, and been the cause of you losing the right to practise your profession.

I've thought a lot about this and Chris will tell you that I am quite calm and determined. I don't want you to think of me as a sort of martyr, either. *I'm* not. I may hate living with Guy again. I will. But *I'd* hate it more if I ruined your life.

I've already phoned Guy and told him I am going back to him. I despise him so much after this last awful thing he's done, somehow it's just shrivelled me up. I don't think I have any more feelings. Even the thought of you doesn't make me cry. *I'm* quite numb. I just want to go right away and make sure you won't be further involved.

For my sake, please, my darling, don't try to follow me or get me back. Nothing will make me change my mind. For the sake of our love and all that has been between us, let it all finish now—on the surface anyhow. I know we will remember each other until we die. For my part you can be sure of that.

Don't try to phone or write. Just leave a tiny note with Chris or Joe which *I'll* pick up some time. And darling Nat, don't be too unhappy. If you really think about it, *you'd* be *in a far worse state if you lost the case eventually and were misjudged and condemned by the G.M.C. and all your medical friends.*

Thank you for the great happiness you gave me. Our week in Mougins will remain in my mind as a sort of heaven I was allowed to enter for a few days. Now it's lost but I'm glad it's all happened and we found each other just for that little while.

This is really goodbye, my darling. It's got to be. By the time you read my letter, I'll be out of England. Guy never does things by halves. He's throwing everything aside and flying with me to Paris later today, and tonight on to South America. It's better that way. You won't feel you must contact me. I think this has been a lesson to Guy anyhow. He wants to keep me and he'll have to behave himself if I stay. But it's only my body he's getting, Nat. My mind and my heart will be yours for ever. I will always adore you. Good-bye, darling, and thank you for loving me."

The signature "*Toni*" was scrawled and smudged but it was there. As definite as the fact that she had gone; that at this hour, 6 p.m. in the evening, she was probably already in France with her husband.

Stricken, dumbfounded, Nat sat there with the letter in his fingers, his eyes staring blindly before him. Toni's sudden departure—her exit from his life—was so final—so absolute—it crushed him. Under normal circumstances he might have torn the letter in half and rushed after her. Then he began to feel resentful. It was monstrous of her to have gone like this—whether she wanted to be a martyr or not, she should have asked him first, he thought in a crazy way. How dared she leave him and go back to that criminal husband of hers? *How dared she?* He'd follow and get her back again. He'd show her whether he was prepared or not to sit back weakly and cancel the divorce, no matter how bloody or rough the result might be. She was the woman he loved. The woman he wanted to marry when all this was over. He wasn't going to let Guy Brand take her—win the battle almost before it had been fought.

Nat sat shaking, sweating, breathing hard and fast.

Then came the second thoughts. The full realisation of what it might have meant if the case had actually come up and Guy had won. Nat had a brief and horrid picture of himself going up before the Medical Council with the inevitable expulsion to follow. The unbelievable horror of knowing that he was no longer allowed to practise medicine. The impact it would have not only upon himself but upon the beloved woman he was living with—married or otherwise. Life could be quite tricky for her in such circumstances.

He realised also that it wasn't the slightest use rushing out of the house to try and find her because he couldn't. Guy would leave no clues as to where he had taken her.

And this time tomorrow she would be, so she said, thousands of miles away.

Nat was no defeatist but it did seem to him now that he would gain nothing by attempting pursuit. He would only make things more difficult for her. He knew Toni. That mixture of strength and weakness. . . God, he thought, how bitterly she had used that strong side today. Leaving him—going back to a man she hated.

And she was doing it for him, *Nat*. Only for him.

It was then that Nat broke. He put his face in his hands and wept, unashamed.

When he was calm again he drank with gratitude the strong whisky Joe had poured out for him. Afterwards he opened the door and called out:

"Chris, Chris, can I speak to you for a moment?"

When she came in, Chris thought she had never seen a man look as ghastly as Nat. Years older. She knew, of course, what Toni had written.

He gave her the faintest smile.

146

"Don't be afraid I'm going to make a fuss. I shall do as Toni wishes. I quite see it's all over."

Chris's heart ached for him—almost as much as it had ached for Toni when they had talked the whole thing out and Toni had taken that grim decision. As long as she lived, Chris would never forget the look in Toni's remarkable eyes as she packed and left Ovington Gardens to go to the penthouse, where Guy was waiting for her.

"She's done a very brave thing—you know that," Chris said.

"Yes, I know. Would it do any good if I managed to trace her and ask her to change her mind?"

"No. If I might say, Nat, I've known Toni longer than you and she's an odd sort of girl. She may appear sometimes to be so helpless and a little vague, but she is very courageous. Once she realised that you would be ruined by this divorce nothing would induce her to turn down Guy's offer. Nothing will bring her back to you now."

Nat turned his face away. He said:

"Can you imagine what I feel—having to stand by and let her do this?"

"I can and I'm dreadfully sorry. Joe and I both think it must be hell for you. We were both, as you know, glad to help you when it all started. But the whole thing has become rather too big to handle, hasn't it?"

"It shouldn't have been."

"It *wouldn't* have been if Guy Brand was not so vicious. Joe and I were both horrified when Toni told us what he'd cooked up. I would never have thought it possible any man would be prepared to go to such lengths to get his revenge."

"He must be mad."

"A lot of people behave in a mad way without being actually insane. The strange thing is that although I have never liked Guy, I've only seen the other side of him up to now and he can be most charming and interesting. He really is schizophrenic."

"And that's the man I'm allowing Toni to live with for the rest of her life?"

"Anything might happen," Chris tried to console him. "It might work out differently. You might even be together again one day. Anyhow you can't do anything now but let Toni go quietly. You'd only make her utterly miserable if you didn't allow her to make her sacrifice."

"Oh, Christ!" said Nat under his breath and turned right away from Chris and stared at the fire.

She looked with pity at the tall lean figure with the bowed shoulders. There was no doubt in her mind at all that this man really loved Toni. To Chris, so happily married, it seemed a tragedy that these two must be the victims of one human being's diabolical wish to hit back—and by unlawful means.

"Would you like another drink?" she asked.

"No thanks. I'll get back home. I've got a lot of thinking to do. I must reorientate my mind. I can't see very straight tonight but I would like to leave a note here for you to give Toni when you are in touch with her again."

"Yes, of course, and *of course* she'll come to see me. We're great friends."

"You've been the greatest," said Nat and held out a hand, "to both of us," he added.

Chris took the hand. What a fine looking man he was, she thought. What a rotten shame that his overwhelming passion for Toni—so warmly returned by her—must end this way.

*   *   *

After Nat left the Masters' home he drove to his consulting room. He still felt stunned. It was almost impossible for him to believe that he would never see Toni again; that all the plans they had built up for their future together had vanished—like Toni herself—into thin air.

I feel as though she's died, he thought.

But it was worse than that. He couldn't even feel that she was removed from the pain and sorrow of life—and God knew she had suffered enough for so young a person. She was very much alive and with *him,* that ghastly sadistic fellow who had driven her almost out of her mind. Nat kept remembering her face—her marvellous eyes—her slim passionately loving body in his arms—her courage and her tremendous thought for him.

He sat at his desk in the quiet room doing nothing—just staring at his blotter. There was an unopened letter on it—his mail was often brought up by the manservant who answered the front door. Finally he opened and read it.

It was from a colleague at the Royal Queenbury outlining the case of a woman whose pregnancy must be terminated due to her heart condition. A case for both Keith and himself. As a rule Nat would have been interested and eager to diagnose. But this evening he found it hard to concentrate. Then a thought struck him. Bigham—the man who was caretaker in the building, answered the front-door and sent patients up to the various consulting rooms used by two other doctors as well as Nat and Lucas-Wright. Would Bigham remember, were he asked, whether or not a Mrs. Guy Brand had ever come here for a consultation?

Then Nat put his face in his hands and shook his head. Too late. No more evidence was needed for the defence. The case wasn't going to be heard. Toni had gone back to Guy.

He went on sitting there in stricken silence. It didn't seem any consolation that he need no longer be afraid of the precious reputation Toni had tried so hard to protect. In fact nothing much mattered to him any more. He wouldn't have cared in this hour whether he was struck off by the G.M.C. or pushed over the edge of a cliff. He felt nothing but a profound misery. He only knew that Toni was in Paris somewhere with that frightful husband of hers and that she'd gone back to save him.

Suddenly, as in Chris's little sitting-room, the tears which Nat might have in the past thought unmanly, began to trickle through his fingers. He said aloud:

"God! God! *God!*"

The telephone bell rang.

Nat pulled himself together and answered the call.

Keith's light tenor voice came over the wires.

"Ah—so you are there, Nat. I hoped I might find you. I've been ringing you at home. I've just taken a chance that you might be at our place. A bit of an emergency has cropped up."

"You mean about Miss Withers' sudden exit?"

As Nat asked the question, he wondered grimly what Lucas-Wright would have said if he had known just *why* Teresa had walked out. That thought was followed by another lightning flash. And secretly and with some pleasure he could presume that that goddamned snake-in-the-grass with her false felonious entries in the appointments' book wouldn't now be getting the fortune she had hoped for. Neither for one moment did he suppose that she could blackmail Guy for more money, because he would have been far too wily to put anything in writing, and neither did she dare admit to the world that she had been an accessory after the fact. Those entries in the book would remain—and who was to care whether Antonia Brand had been his patient or not.

"Nat—are you there?" came Keith's sharp voice.

"Oh sorry—yes, of course. What is it, Keith?"

"Nothing to do with Teresa. We can replace her. But I want you, if you possibly can, to join me straightaway at the Clinic. A patient of mine has been admitted and it has only just evolved that part of her condition is due to..."

There followed various gynaecological details which Nat jotted down on the pad in front of him. Keith ended:

"It may mean an emergency operation with both of us there. Incidentally, it's the actress Veryan Grey. I think I told you, she came to see me once about her heart."

"Yes, I remember."

Everybody knew Veryan Grey. Beautiful, talented, fortyish and not very long married to a famous dramatic critic.

"Can you come at once?" asked Keith.

"Yes, of course."

Nat put down the receiver. He lit a cigarette, smoked it for a second or two, then extinguished it. Opening one of the windows, he squared his shoulders and drew in several deep draughts of the night air. He could hear a church bell striking the hour. Seven o'clock. Lights were shining from the windows of the great metropolis.

Life had to go on. Death was his old enemy, thought Nat, and only a short while ago he had been wondering how to fight Guy Brand in order to be allowed to carry on with the battle.

He was suddenly glad that an emergency had arisen and he could throw himself into his work. He must try to forget Toni—for a little while anyhow. He closed the window, switched off his table lamp and walked out to the lift.

15

The air hostess who looked after the V.I.P. passengers on the Boeing, bent over Toni. She was sitting with her head back and her eyes closed. Such a gorgeous-looking girl, the hostess had thought when Mrs. Brand first came on board. And what a mink coat! But she didn't like the girl's colour at the moment.

"Are you all right, Mrs Brand?" she asked anxiously. "Not feeling bad?"

Toni's lashes lifted. Oh, what eyes, the hostess thought, but she really did look ill and not very happy.

"Sure you aren't feeling a bit sick?"

"No," said Toni, "I'm perfectly all right."

"Can I ask the steward to bring you a brandy before we settle down for the night?"

Toni gave her a faint grateful smile but shook her head.

"No, I'm quite all right, really. I'm always rather pale."

The girl moved away. Toni sat motionless. Beside her, Guy put away his cigar.

"Perhaps this is upsetting you. I won't smoke any more."

"Please do. I'm perfectly all right," she repeated.

"Well, try and get some sleep once they dim the lights, my dear. You've got a long night's flying before you."

"Thank you, Guy."

"I really do hope you're not feeling ill," he added on a genuine note of solicitude.

Now she turned and looked at him. He was startled by the sheer loathing in those magnificent eyes. Not for the first time since this whole thing had blown up he felt uneasy. He knew that he had behaved outrageously. Sadist though he was, Guy Brand normally acted as a reputable citizen and with a great deal more good sense than he had shown out of his hideous wish to persecute Toni and ruin her lover (that damned doctor!). Yet why should he, Guy, feel any regrets over the thing he had tried to do? Hadn't Nathaniel Olver committed adultery with Guy Brand's wife? Olver would have deserved what came to him had the scheme gone through. As for Toni, she had been unfaithful and wounded Guy's pride beyond bearing. He had suffered horribly, believing that he had lost his dearly prized wife.

Now it was ended. But he experienced a certain embarrassment at the thought of what he had done in order to get his revenge. It had been a criminal act. He had at moments recoiled at the idea of dealing with a cheap unscrupulous couple like Miss Withers and her fancy-man.

When Toni had walked into the penthouse back into his life, she looked a stranger to him in her unfamiliar clothes and he had at first wanted to hurt her all over again—punish her for what she had done to him. But the sadistic instincts had turned to unaccustomed emotion. He greeted her warmly, assured her that he would never mention the past to her again and that she must try to forget it all. He had, he told her, literally dreaded the idea of telling everybody that she had run away from him. He'd been driven almost beyond endurance so she must forgive his subsequent behaviour. To him, Antonia's departure was as terrible as though a thief had broken into the penthouse and removed his Renoir—the exquisite painting that gave him the deepest satisfaction.

But deeper than his desire to let the divorce go through and to use his false evidence against Olver, was his wish to get Toni back. To see her in all her grace and beauty moving around his home, entertaining his guests, receiving the burning, desirous glances of the other men who could never possess her.

In his twisted, tormented mind, Guy wanted her as no other

man on earth could want. He was obsessed by her—all the more so because he had been unable to break her spirit even while he succeeded in bruising and torturing her mind.

He had felt both surprised and delighted when she first told him she would go back to him if he dropped the divorce and left her lover's name out of the whole affair. Nevertheless there had been bad moments for Guy, especially when he contacted Teresa Withers and told her that he would not be in touch with her again because the case was being dropped and his wife was returning to him.

First of all, Teresa had screamed her fury and resentment. Then her boy-friend had taken over and tried to threaten Guy. Blackmail, of course.

"We'll make it so hot for you, you won't be able to stay in London unless you send the rest of the money to Geneva," Rod had shouted.

But Guy had a ready answer.

"One word from you and I shall put the police on you for threatening me. You can never prove that we had any kind of agreement. And don't forget, if *I* am indicted you will be sent to prison as accessories after the fact. You'd go up for a few years—for receiving money to be used for criminal purposes. You've had your two hundred and fifty—it's more than either of you deserve. Now don't let me hear another sound from you."

He didn't suppose that he ever would. It was unlikely that either Miss Withers or her boy-friend wished to face imprisonment just for the sake of making things unpleasant for *him;* they were not going to get another penny, no matter what they did.

Toni made it clear to Guy that Nat had no intention of continuing with his own litigation, or accusing Teresa of falsifying the appointment book. It was all pointless now.

So here they were—Mr. and Mrs. Guy Brand flying to Brazil like a happily married couple.

Guy had formerly enjoyed himself in Rio. He believed

that the sunshine and glamour of Brazil would bring some colour back into Toni's cheeks. Even he, who was hardly a sympathetic man, had felt a trifle disconcerted by her appearance when he saw her again. She looked as though he had beaten her to death.

He said:

"Aren't you going to speak to me, Antonia?"

She looked at him icily.

"I've come back," she said, "that must be enough for the moment."

"It's going to be a pretty dreary holiday if we're not going to have any conversation," he muttered, and lifted the brandy-and-soda the steward had just given him to his lips.

"I'm sorry," said Toni. "For the moment I absolutely cannot communicate with you. Please leave me alone. Give me time."

He shrugged his shoulders.

Then suddenly as though a knife had gone through her mind, Toni turned on him. She spoke in a low voice and with such bitterness and contempt that even Guy was shaken.

"You've done a lot of terrible things to me but when I think what you tried to do to *Nat*, I'm filled with such revulsion that I want to be sick—yes, *sick!*"

He began to bluster:

"I only behaved like any outraged husband would do and—"

"Oh, no," she broke in. "We've had this out. I know you. You got hold of that secretary woman and used her miserable obsession for her penniless boy-friend in order to bribe her. You made her put that false entry in the appointment book."

"You can't prove it."

"Maybe not and it doesn't matter now, but *I* know about it; and it was a great deal worse than my—my *adultery*."

Guy drained his glass and began to chew at his lower lip. He didn't feel too pleased. This was a Toni he had never had to deal with before. This was not the soft frightened little girl with the big eyes and tender mouth. She had changed in quite a fantastic way. He wasn't at all sure he didn't regret asking her to return. Perhaps he didn't want her so much after all. Perhaps he had over-rated her desirability. But it was too late. In bringing her away like this, he had condoned the whole affair. Oh well, Guy tried to console himself, no doubt she'd get over it and over her ill-feeling toward him—in time. Yes, as she had said, he must give her time. He put in a final plea for himself.

"After all, I'm sure I must have shown how much I wanted you back with me, Antonia. It wasn't at all convenient for me to leave London at a moment's notice like this. I shall probably lose business over it. I don't mind so long as I know you appreciate my wish to please you. I knew you wouldn't want to stay in England just now."

Toni had to drag her thoughts back to him. They had drifted on to another level. She was seeing the shocked haggard face of the man she loved more than anyone else when he first read that damning letter from Guy's solicitors. She remembered the whole frightful business.

"Antonia, did you hear what I said?" asked Guy.

"Yes. But I'm not interested. Please let me sleep."

He shrugged his shoulders.

When Toni looked at him again she saw that Guy was asleep. Her lips curled. How contemptible he was! Not for a moment did she wish to exonerate her own original action in having taken a lover.

But, she thought, *if there is a God, He knows what I went through with Guy and knows how much I love Nat. Surely He will forgive me.*

Now the lights in the great aircraft were dimmed. Most of the passengers reclined on their cushions and were dozing, as the Boeing moved with fantastic speed under the cold light of a million stars.

Toni suddenly heard the voice of an American woman, in the seat on the other side of her. Still awake and being chatty.

"Say, lover-boy—it's going to be mighty fine in Rio. Think of the sun again after all that darned weather in little old England. We're going to have a swell time together."

The man answered:

"Life's always mighty swell with you, baby."

Toni shut her eyes. Lucky woman. But life had been 'mighty swell' for Toni in Mougins. Dear little Mougins, did it really exist? And lovely *Mas Candille;* their sweet lovely bedroom, looking down into the valley and up the mountainside to the twinkling lights of Grasse; and all the exultation she had experienced of being alive, warm and secure in Nat's arms.

Secure?

Dear God, how insecure she had been, and how crazy to suppose there was any such thing as safety for illicit lovers!

A sudden lurch in the big Boeing brought Guy's heavy body closer to hers; then as the aircraft righted itself and sped on toward Madrid, Toni shrank as far as she could get away from Guy's hateful flesh.

Suddenly, for the first time since she left Chris's home, and took that taxi to River Court, the tears began to flow, forcing their way under her shut lids and rolling down her cheeks, painful, scalding tears. Soundlessly she cried for her lost love and her vanished happiness. Exhausted though she was, she could not sleep. But she tried to concentrate on the thought of Nat going off to the Royal Queenbury in the morning. At least his cherished profession was secure at last.

She was sure that he would be unhappy for a while. Perhaps he would always love and regret her. She was quite certain that if she had given him the chance he would have tried to stop her from making this sacrifice for him. Nevertheless Toni, with a cynicism she used not to feel, wondered whether he wouldn't in time be thankful that their love affair had ended. She must make a special effort to let him know, through Chris, that all was well with her, or he would be worried.

Tired and unhappy though she was, Toni had made up her mind to let neither sorrow nor pain destroy her. For if anything happened to her it would react upon Nat. He would feel responsible. Then what she had done wouldn't have been worth while.

On this long agonising flight to Rio—knowing that every mile they covered was taking her further and further away from Nat, and all the joy she had known with him, Toni felt that she was shut for ever now in impenetrable darkness. She felt terribly lonely. This man at her side, this tyrant who had been willing to do Nat such a terrible wrong rather than lose her, could never in her mind seem anything but an enemy. There could be no friendship between them. Solitude was possibly the sharpest misery Toni had to bear. Yet the further she flew, the stronger she felt. The old feebleness had left her for always. She needed this new strength, God alone knew, she thought, if she was to stay with Guy.

She kept remembering all that had happened when she faced him once again in the hot flower-filled luxurious penthouse which had never held any welcome or charm for her and which in that moment held still less. It was like a tomb.

Guy was not quite the self-important, confident man she had left. He made pretence at appearing so but she knew by the way he tugged at his collar and kept wiping his perspiring forehead and laughing nervously now and then, that he was far from easy in his mind.

He said:

"I must make up to you for all this—er—nonsense about you falling for your—er—surgeon. I'm going to be magnanimous and call it just an infatuation and forget all about it." Those were his first words.

Toni looked him straight in the eyes—a look of utter scorn.

"Forget it, then. I don't want to hear about it. And don't try to be generous, please. What *can't* be forgotten is your sordid efforts to wreck a surgeon's reputation."

Guy turned away, obviously unwilling to face her.

"I've got some champagne on ice—let's have it," he said, clearing his throat.

"Keep it—I don't want it."

He turned to her, red and blustering.

"I think *you've* got something to be ashamed of, haven't you—" he began. "Why this haughty attitude, Antonia?"

"I refuse to feel ashamed. Whatever I did you asked for. I came back to you on the understanding that we would not have a scene about it. I just can't take any more. If you say another word I'll walk out for good this time."

He covered his confusion by lighting a cigar. He shrugged his wide shoulders. Toni was certainly no longer a timid young girl with that quaint Victorian quality of shyness and innocence that had attracted him when he first met her in Paris. He began to wish quite sincerely that he had not behaved so badly. He'd been a bit off his head when Toni first ran away, or he would never have stooped so low.

He tried another line.

"Let's begin again, Antonia—a new life together. I mean— get rid of all your old clothes, sell your old jewellery, if you like; choose something quite new. I'll buy you anything you like. I swear I'll try to please you."

By then she was standing at the window looking across the river, her gaze fixed, stony. She wished in the depths of her mind that she could have thrown herself into that water and let it close over her head so that she need never see Guy's plump face, or hear his throaty succulent voice again. But she was not the suicide type, added to which she didn't think it right for any human being to take his own life. *And* if she did such a thing it would be appalling for Nat. He would blame himself.

She said:

"You haven't learned yet, Guy, that I'm not interested in your presents and if we're going to begin again then please just leave me in peace. I'm absolutely exhausted and want breathing space."

He suggested quite humbly that she should go and rest until it was time for her to dress and pack for the night flight to Brazil.

She left him and locked herself in her bedroom. She was shaking with nerves and fatigue. She hadn't the slightest wish to go to Rio but she did at least feel grateful to Guy for quitting his work at a moment's notice in order to take her so far away. She knew that she couldn't have borne it if she had had to stay here in this flat tonight with Guy, knowing that Nat was only a mile or two away.

*   *   *

Now in the Boeing, sleepless, still desperately tired, she was well aware that it didn't much matter where she was. The whole great world could be be whittled down to the size of a walnut when it came to one's thoughts, one's feelings. They were ever present. Nat was here, beside her. He would always be beside her.

She tried to concentrate on the memory of the marvellous moments they had had together. He had been so utterly kind and good—gay and full of love of her—she'd been lucky to know him, to have been loved by him. She shut her eyes and went on remembering.

So the long night and the long flight passed. Sheer physical fatigue finally blotted out her thoughts. She slept for an hour before they landed for refuelling.

When Guy took the trouble to point out the exceptional beauty and splendour of Rio harbour as they flew over it, she tried to appear interested. She tried also to make up her mind how best to deal with Guy. She dared not look too far into the future, but she couldn't maintain a constant embittered enmity and continually express her hatred and contempt for him. No marriage could survive that. Unhappily she must make sure *this* marriage did survive for quite a long time, *if* she wanted to preserve her own sanity and keep Guy to his promise to leave Nat alone. She knew Guy too well not to be sure he would ever really change for the better. He might try to give her more freedom and not subject her to his former attempts to corrupt her mind and her body. But he would eventually fall back and become the old Guy.

Having said goodbye to Nat, the worst bitterness was past for her. Now, really, she told herself, anything more that she had to do would seem trivial. As long as she could keep her personal integrity, she could ask little more and she must in return be polite at least to Guy and make some effort to take her place in public as his wife.

She began to feel a very great deal further from Nat once they were in the sumptuous suite in Rio, in the Copacabana Palace Hotel, after a rest and a meal. She began to realise that she had brought only a small suitcase with her. Reluctant though she was to do so she could not refuse Guy when he suggested she went out to buy some summer clothes. It was very hot here.

When she told Guy that she wished to go out alone, he protested. She quickly put an end to that.

"I *want* to be alone, Guy. I assure you I'm not going to run away from you. You don't have to behave as though you are a jailer."

"Oh, very well," he said rather unwillingly.

"I'll be back in say a couple of hours' time," she said.

*   *   *

Later the little chambermaid who called herself Juanita helped Toni unpack all the boxes that she brought back in the car Guy had hired with chauffeur. As she pulled the lovely summer dresses and coats and lingerie from their folds of tissue paper, the girl uttered ecstatic exclamations.

"Oh—beautiful! The Senhora has such gorgeous things. The Senhor is so generous; so handsome; the Senhora is so lucky!"

Toni sat at her dressing-table mechanically filing her nails while she listened to this chatter. She smiled at the pretty dark-haired girl.

"You speak good English."

"I work with English and American tourists. I learn, and I have boy-friend speaka English."

"Are you going to be married soon?"

"I hope, Senhora. *Mucha*—I hope."

"You are very much—in love?"

"Very, very, and he is, too. Very happy—" Juanita giggled— her eyes sparkling at Toni. Now she opened a box and pulled out a gold gauzy shawl with a long fringe. It shimmered as the girl held it up.

"Oh, *magnifico!* I like!"

"You can have it," said Toni indifferently.

The girl gasped.

"*Have* ... gold shawl? ... no, no, *impossible!*"

"Take it, I can buy another."

The emotional Brazilian girl rushed to Toni, seized her hand and kissed it, calling down the blessing of the Virgin Mary upon the Senhora. Never, never had Juanita received such a magnificent present. She would keep it for her wedding the so-precious golden shawl.

After the girl had left and Toni was alone, she folded her arms on the dressing-table and leaned her forehead against them.

Oh, God, how wonderful it would be just to find herself a little chambermaid with a fond lover she could marry soon— and to whom the gift of a gold fringed shawl should mean so much. Once again, Toni felt utterly forsaken—in prison—

surrounded by cupboards filled with extravagant things in this room with a door that led into another—where a man who revolted her, waited.

She shuddered and pulled herself together. She had sworn not to let this sort of bitterness accumulate. She must get on top of it.

Oh, Nat, where are you? What are you doing at this moment? Are you thinking about me as I am about you? Oh, Nat, you are thousands of miles away now and I shall never, never see you again.

Guy walked into the room. He was immaculately dressed as usual in a light-weight pale grey suit, and wearing a button-hole. He looked quite gay.

"I've been lucky, my dear. There's a very special concert on tonight, and I've managed to get a box. You like good music, I know."

"Thank you," Toni said with an effort, but kept her back turned to him.

"Have you unpacked all your new purchases?"

"Yes. Thank you for—for giving me so much to spend. They have gorgeous shops here. The little maid was quite overcome just now."

"But you don't care a damn for anything, do you?" he asked with sudden bitterness, and stared at her gloomily.

She was wearing a short white silk dressing-gown tied with a wide sash which made her waist look very slender. A cloud of dark hair half concealed her face. Her delicate legs were bare to the thighs. He felt the old unhealthy desire to break down her defiant spirit, to hurt her *somehow*. To hell with that martyr attitude—she was no saint! Dammit, she'd been unfaithful to him, hadn't she? What was she being so high and mighty about?

All that was low and vile in Guy simmered dangerously on the surface but Toni held him with her rigid gaze. Those golden eyes were ice-cold, and there was a warning in them that kept him from laying a finger on her.

He mopped at his face, muttering that the humidity in here was terrible, and he must switch the air conditioning on higher. Then he left her.

I wonder, thought Toni despairingly, *how long I shall have to live with him like this.*

That night, after the concert, they had food at an exclusive restaurant where Guy ran into Peter Sinclair—one of his English friends in the Diplomatic Service, and his wife. They had drinks together—a gay, talkative supper. On their way back to their apartment, Mrs. Sinclair said:

"Peter, did you ever *see* such a beautiful girl as Mrs. Brand?"

"Never—gorgeous eyes!" he nodded.

"And that emerald ring—her jewels were fabulous. You said he was a millionaire, didn't you? He's very good-looking, too, though a bit on the heavy side. He seems to adore her. Some women are lucky."

16

The Brands stayed in Brazil for over two weeks, going from Rio to Buenos Aires and then back to Rio, meeting many of Guy's wealthy business connections as well as personal friends.

It was a hectic time. Hot sunny days; trips to the sea; sunbathing, swimming, water ski-ing, all that the rich could be offered in a very rich country. Wherever Toni went, she was a success. That strangely elusive, unique quality in her beauty and her delicate slender body fascinated people. Guy was frankly delighted by the flattery she received and the congratulations that were offered him. He told her so repeatedly. She made no answer but thought with irony that Guy was getting exactly what he wanted now that he had her back. She was once again the star in his firmament—the possession he valued most.

There were times when he tried to revert to being the vicious tyrant of the past but Toni had put up a barrier between them now that he could not break. She had become inaccessible, and for the time anyhow, he had to allow her to remain so. Not that he intended that it should always be this way. But for just now she had the upper hand. He did not wish to lose her and he dared not risk her leaving him again.

She flung herself into most of the amusements and distractions that were offered, because she found it easier when she had no time to brood over the past. But there were moments when the need to contact Nat was so devastating, she hardly knew how to stand it.

Darling Chris, her faithful friend—the one person who

must know what she was going through—had written twice. The letters had followed and found her. On both occasions Chris told her that she had telephoned Nat (as requested by Toni) to say that she was well and that he need not worry about her. Nat had asked that a similar message should be sent to Toni. He, too, was well and hard at work.

Both of us are liars, Toni thought, with tremendous bitterness, *it wouldn't do for us to speak the truth*.

At the end of those two weeks in Brazil, it was suggested by Guy that they should go home.

"You needn't stay in London if you don't want to. You can go down to Bray and I'll join you at weekends," he said, "but I must get back to the office."

She was silent for a moment. She had no wish to return to England but she could see that it was not fair to keep Guy away from his job any longer. She agreed to fly home. But she dreaded it. She couldn't see Nat while she was all this way away from home. Once in London ... oh, God, it was going to be so hard not to pick up that telephone! On the other hand, she was sick of all the parties and dinners and the constant efforts Guy made to amuse her. If he would really let her live alone for the best part of the week in their river home she would prefer it. At this time of the year—early November—it would be damp and foggy down there, but anything would be better than living in town, cheek by jowl with Guy all the time.

He on his part had to stifle his raging desire to break down the present barrier between them. In consequence, he grew sullen and dissatisfied—and a new feeling toward Toni began to grow in him—something even stronger than his old desire for possession. A savage resentment because she had defeated him, and because he knew that she was still fretting for that other man.

He even began to wish that he could have carried out his dastardly plan to get Olver struck off by the General Medical Council.

On the day before they left Rio, Toni developed a sick headache which kept her from going with Guy to an exhibition of paintings after which they were to have been entertained in the private home of one of the great Brazilian collectors. Nothing would have induced Guy to cancel such an appointment, neither did Toni wish him to.

"You go," said Toni. "Make my excuses."

Guy looked into the beautiful unsmiling eyes and wondered when in fact, he had last seen her smile.

"You hate me, don't you?" he asked with sudden uncontrolled anger.

"Do you expect me to love you?"

"Oh, go to hell!" he said and slammed the communicating door between them.

She was thankful when he left the hotel. It was good to be alone. She lay in bed, hot and restless, although sunblinds shaded the room. She put a handkerchief soaked in *eau-de-toilet* across her aching brow and tried to sleep. Tried not to think of Nat.

What a lot one could suffer, yet go on appearing to others as though one hadn't a care in the world, she thought.

She looked at the ivory telephone on the bed beside her. How tormenting to think that she could lift that receiver and tell the operator to get a line to England—to Nat—and that she would be able to hear him speak. But to what purpose? It would only upset them both. She tried to laugh aloud, but it had a cracked sound. Maybe, she thought, Nat would tell her that he was learning at last to do without her. Or perhaps there was somebody new to console him. Somebody he could marry in time.

Toni turned her face to the pillow and soaked it with her scalding tears.

*   *   *

Suddenly the telephone bell rang, startling her. More than

possibly it was for Guy, but when she answered, the operator asked her to hold on. It was a person-to-person call from London for Mrs. Brand.

"Are you sure it isn't for *Mr*. Brand?" asked Toni.

"No Senhora, it is for *Mrs*. Antonia Brand."

Toni's pulse-rate quickened. She had a sort of fatalistic feeling that this call was either from Nat or about him. Then she heard Chris's familiar voice.

"Toni, is that you?"

"Yes, hullo, Chris darling. What a surprise! Marvellous to hear you."

"Can I speak, or is Guy there?"

"No, he's out. Go ahead."

"I'm afraid I have bad news for you."

Toni's heart plunged down, down, into fear.

"*Bad news?* You mean ... Nat ... ?"

"Yes, I'm afraid so."

Toni broke out into a cold sweat. She gripped the receiver more tightly.

"Oh, God, *what?*"

Then a woman's voice speaking in Portuguese cut across the line. Chris's voice receded. Panting, Toni called the operator.

"Are you there? Are you there? I've been cut off."

"Are you wanting me, Senhora?" asked the hotel operator blandly.

"Yes. I've been cut off ... the most urgent call ... it was from London ... please connect me again at once."

"You must put down your receiver, Senhora. You did not make the call. I am sorry but no doubt they will come back soon."

With a shaking hand, Toni put the instrument back on its stand. How damnable to be cut off before Chris could explain. *Oh God*, she thought, *bad news about Nat. Oh, Nat, Nat, don't tell me something's happened to you!*

She got up, and sat on the edge of the bed, shaking. Her

whole body felt hot and damp. She sat staring at the telephone as though willing it to speak. Then the bell rang again, and with feverish haste she grabbed the receiver and answered.

Now she could hear Chris again, very clearly for such a long distance call.

"Nat's had an accident."

"What? Tell me, quickly."

"In a car."

"The Triumph?"

"No. He was in a Mercedes-Benz with another doctor—going to see a patient of his—on Western Avenue on the way to Gerrards Cross. It happened soon after they passed the White City and were on the open road. This doctor—I don't know his name—tried to pass something and misjudged the speed of another car coming toward him. It was a head-on crash."

"Is—Nat dead?"

Toni asked the question with a kind of croak in her voice but Chris heard it.

"No. The driver got the full impact, poor man. He died on the way to hospital. Nat was thrown forward on the windscreen; he wasn't wearing a belt, unfortunately. His head was badly injured. He's still unconscious in Hammersmith Hospital."

Toni dug the points of her finger nails into the palms of both her shaking hands. She kept feeling that there was something in her throat that kept her from speaking clearly.

"How ... bad ... is he?"

A pause. In terror Toni shouted another question:

"Can you hear me, Chris? *How bad is he?*"

"I must tell you the truth, darling. He's on the danger list."

Another pause. Toni sat still, gripping the telephone, feeling as though the world was crashing around her. A dreadful sickness of both mind and body had seized her. Somehow she managed to carry on the conversation with Chris.

"You mean he may—die?"

169

"There's always a chance he won't—" began Chris.

Toni broke in:

"No, he's going to die. I know it. I shall come back at once. I've got to be with him. I don't care what Guy says or does. I've got to be with Nat if it's the last thing I do."

"Do you think you ought?—" Chris began again but Toni interrupted:

"I'll get the first possible flight. God knows when I'll arrive, but go and see him, Chris—tell him he must hang on. He *must* hang on till I come."

"Ring me up when you arrive at Heathrow," said Chris.

An English voice cut in:

"Your three minutes are up, caller, do you wish to continue?"

It was Toni who put down the receiver. She had nothing more to say but a great deal to do.

It was very quiet in her big luxurious bedroom except for the faint music of a rhumba band from a distant radio.

Now Toni was calm. Nothing seemed to matter except that she should see Nat—speak to him once more before he died.

"Oh, my love," she kept saying, *"Oh, my poor love!"*

It was intolerable to think that Nat with all his gifts—his ability to help suffering humanity, his charm, his vigour, his wit—must die at so young an age. But this was no time for nostalgia—for remembering their love and their happiness together. She only knew that he mattered more to her than her own life. Guy didn't matter. He wouldn't be able to hurt Nat.

She dressed quickly, then called the operator and asked to be put through to the Airport.

She could not transfer her ticket. Guy had made the bookings through his agent. Toni didn't care. Recklessly she asked for the next possible flight and found that it would be at 9.40 this evening, reaching Heathrow at 3.45 the following day.

She booked it and promised to be at the Airport to collect and pay for the ticket at least three hours before. This would give her time to see Guy and get some money from him. If he refused to give her the fare, she would sell the emerald ring or borrow on it from the hotel manager.

*   *   *

By the time Guy came home she had packed and was sitting quite ready in the sitting-room of their suite. She was still in a thin dress and jacket because it was so hot. But she had her mink coat beside her. She knew it would be cold when they touched down at Heathrow.

She remembered how she had left everything behind her when she first ran away from Guy. Tonight she had no such compunction. She might need both the coat and the ring to sell and she was going to use them. After the atrocious way he had behaved—during the early days of their marriage as well as later on—he owed her something.

Guy, flushed from the champagne his Brazilian friends had given him, was in a good humour when finally he walked into their room. He spoke to Toni jovially.

"Are you feeling better, my dear?"

Then he saw the mink coat she was wearing and the two cases beside her. His smile vanished. He stared.

"What in the name of—"

He got no further but went on staring, dumbfounded.

She faced him—without fear. She had never felt stronger. The sickness that had almost overcome her when she first heard the news about Nat was gone. She hadn't even bothered to make up her face. But she stood before Guy with squared shoulders, and calm resolution in her tragic eyes.

"I've heard from England that Nat has been involved in a serious accident. He's dying. I'm going to him," she said in a loud clear voice.

Guy's heavy face reddened.

"You must be out of your mind. I . . . of course I'm sorry your boy-friend's dying—but you have no right to go to him.

You're my wife."

"You have no right to dictate to *me*, and I shall not be your wife much longer. When Nat is gone, I shall live alone. This time I'm leaving you for good and never coming back. There's nothing whatsoever you can do to hurt either him or me."

Guy was reduced to silence. A look of almost ludicrous surprise and dismay replaced his usually arrogant, self-confident expression. He began to stammer:

"Oh, look here—you can't do this to me, Antonia. You promised to come back and—"

"And I came," she broke in, "but it was blackmail. You know I would never have done it if you hadn't tried to buy that false testimony against Nat, and take such hideous advantage of the fact that he was a doctor. Now—you can do nothing to him. The last thing in the world I want is to go on living with you. I hate the very sight of you. I despise you for everything you have done to both of us. So our marriage is ended."

"Look here—" Guy began to bluster again.

"I'm only going to ask you one more thing in this life," she added, "and that's for enough money to pay for my ticket. I managed to get a cancellation on the Boeing. I'm going to drive to the Airport in a few moments and stay there until I fly. I'd rather be there alone than here with you."

The terrible loathing in her voice and her eyes seemed suddenly to deflate Guy in a manner which Toni would never have thought possible. He sat down heavily and began to breathe in a noisy way. He kept stammering; trying to excuse himself.

"I don't see why you should act this way, Antonia. I haven't always behaved as well as I should, but you've never tried to see my side of things. You've never been the sort of wife I expected. I couldn't do with all that romanticism you go in for or begin to give you the sort of love you wanted. You wouldn't even meet me half-way."

"No decent woman could meet you half-way, Guy, but please don't let's waste time in recriminations. The man I love and wanted to be with, is dying, so I'm going to him and I shall stay until—he dies. Nothing can stop me. If you won't give me my fare—I'll sell the emerald. If there's no time to go to a jeweller, then I'll ask the manager to take either the ring or my mink—just for the price of my ticket. I'm quite sure he'd willingly do that. It's worth thousands."

Guy coughed and dabbed at his lips with his handkerchief.

"There's no need for you to throw away your mink in such a silly fashion—or sell the emerald."

She drew the ring from her finger.

"Take it then and please exchange it for the price of my fare."

The offer of the fabulous jewel was too much for Guy. He was mercenary to the core. He took the ring, shrugging.

"Very well, if you insist on behaving in this idiotic way. Here is more than enough for your ticket."

He took a clipped pile of banknotes from his wallet and handed them to her.

"Thank you," she said coldly and put them in her bag.

He came nearer her.

"Antonia—there's no need to treat me quite so badly. I've done a hell of a lot for you. You were a little nobody when I met you."

She drew back. Her face was drawn; her eyes underlined with suffering. It didn't really seem to matter much what Guy was saying. Her mind kept darting to the memory of Nat—unconscious, on the danger list, lying in Hammersmith Hospital. It would be awful if she were too late to find him alive—to be unable to tell him once more how much she loved him. She said:

"I've never wanted your presents, Guy. When I married

173

you, I thought I loved you. I hoped to find love in return—as any normal girl would. You can't possibly justify what you did to me. You just can't, so don't try. The only mistake I made was in staying with you so long."

He looked at her gloomily.

That he had lost her now, finally and absolutely, was plain. It was the first and only time in his life that Guy Brand had had to admit defeat. Suddenly he swung from magnanimity to sullen indifference.

"Go and be damned," he said, "I've had about enough of you. I don't know why I went to such ridiculous lengths to keep you. You'll regret this, Antonia. You won't find it easy to replace a man like myself. But I shall find it only too easy to replace you. There are thousands of beautiful attractive women in the world who would find *me* attractive too, you know."

"I'm sure there are. You can be so charming. But there's the other side of the coin. I can think of no sort of woman who would enjoy discovering that."

He clenched his hands.

"Oh, get out and this time, stay out of my life," he snarled at her. "And whether your boy-friend lives or not—I couldn't care less."

She began to walk toward the door, the coat over her arm, one case in her hand.

"Good-bye, Guy. I hope I never see you again."

"Get out!" he shouted.

They were the last words she heard from him.

*   *   *

After that she was very much alone. The long agonising flight back to London began. After take-off, she leaned back in her seat and shut her eyes. She stayed like that, motionless, dazed, half dead after the battering she had received. She didn't often pray but she prayed now.

God don't let Nat die until I've seen him again. Don't, please!

After it was all over, everything would be over for her, too. But at least she could be thankful that she had taken this step and put Guy out of her life for ever. At least she wouldn't have to take any more punishment from him—in payment for her defence of Nat.

The flight seemed endless—first the stop to refuel at Madrid, then moving rapidly through the morning light and on to Paris in the noon. Only then did she begin to feel that she was near—very near to Nat again.

17

The great Boeing touched down at Heathrow Airport on time. They came through heavy cloud. It was pouring with rain and bitterly cold in London after Rio de Janeiro. Toni was glad of the mink coat. And now that she was back in England—so much nearer to him—her strength, her purpose, intensified. As soon as she was through Customs she rushed to a telephone-box and called Chris. Her first anguished question was:

"Is he all right?"

"Still unconscious," was the reply.

"He's still alive?"

"Yes. Is Guy with you?"

"No—I'm alone. I've left him this time for good."

"I don't blame you. Joe was only saying to me the other day that man deserves anything that's coming to him after what he tried to do."

Toni wasted no more time. She hired a car and drove up to London—straight to the Hammersmith hospital.

The Sister-in-charge of the private room where Nat had been taken was human and helpful and very kind to the lovely girl in the lovely coat. She looked so dreadfully tired Sister thought; had such heavy shadows under her eyes, poor thing.

Sister made haste to answer the first agonised question.

"He's still very ill and the doctors can't, of course, say anything definite. But he is young and has a strong heart—that helps."

"May I see him?"

The Sister looked at her gravely. She knew that Mr. Olver was not married. They all knew about Mr. Olver. His fame was widespread. His work at the Royal Queenbury was often mentioned in medical journals. He had been brought in here as an accident casualty because the crash had occurred such a short distance away. But already half a dozen or more of the doctors from the Queenbury who were his friends had called. His private room was full of flowers which he had not yet seen.

Sister was a woman of the world and not, as she hoped, too much of a 'square'. If this was Mr. Olver's special girl-friend she must be afforded some attention. To be sure, she was a gorgeous-looking girl.

Then Toni began:

"Quite confidentially, Sister, Mr. Olver and I—"

"You needn't say any more, my dear," broke in the other woman, "I understand."

So Toni was taken into Nat's private room. She did not even notice the flowers. She saw only Nat's face, still slightly tanned against the whiteness of the bandages which were capped about his skull and across his forehead. There were two strips of plaster on one side of his nose and across the left high cheek-bone. He lay so still that Toni's whole heart seemed to shrink.

"Oh, Nat, *Nat!*" she whispered.

Sister took her arm.

"He won't be able to hear or see you. It's no use you staying really. Come back tomorrow. He may recover consciousness soon. I promise to let you know."

Toni accepted this. Her eyes swam now with the tears she had been unable to shed since she first heard about the accident. She stumbled into the corridor and back to the waiting room where she talked to the Sister for a few more moments.

"You do think he'll be all right—that he won't die?" she kept asking piteously.

"My dear, I simply cannot give you a straight answer. I can only tell you that the doctors still hope, and he is receiving every attention. He has a special nurse—that tall girl you saw going in just now, as we came out. He's being watched all the time."

"I'll go to my friends," said Toni in a muffled voice, "but if he does open his eyes at all and can understand, will you *please* tell him that—*Toni* is back, and will stay with him, and that there's nothing more for him to worry about."

"I promise to give him that message, Miss—er."

"Mrs. Brand," Toni finished for her, reluctantly.

"I won't forget."

"And if I give you my telephone-number will you ring me the moment he does recover or alternatively—" her voice broke. She could go on no further.

*   *   *

Once back in the familiar little maisonette in Ovington Gardens, the last shred of Toni's strength and courage seemed to desert her. In Chris's loving and understanding arms, she sobbed out her grief and her pain. Chris kept smoothing the long silky hair, comforting her as she would have done her child.

"Don't despair. He'll be all right, I'm sure he will, darling. Keep your chin up."

It took her a long time to quieten Toni, then Chris put her to bed with a strong sedative.

"You need some sleep, my girl, and if you don't get it, you won't be fit to go to the hospital when you *are* wanted."

Those words had effect. So did the sleeping pill. Toni slept for most of that night without waking. Chris tip-toed into the spare room to see her several times. On the last occasion Chris returned to the warmth and comfort of her husband's arms and almost dissolved into tears herself.

"My God, what that girl has had to suffer. Oh, Joe, how lucky I am to be with you."

"We're both lucky," said Joe, "but I must say this Toni-Guy affair has been one hell of a ruddy drama."

"Drama!" repeated Chris, snuggling her face against his neck. "*Melo*drama, the way things have been going. I hope to God Nat doesn't die. It'll just about kill her if he does."

"And what if he lives? What's that ruddy fellow going to do to them next?"

"Nothing if you ask me. I have an idea he's regretted his grim effort to smash up Nat's career, and quite frankly, darling, the way Toni's been acting I don't see why Guy should want to hang on to her any longer. Even if he's a sadist, there must be a limit to his oddness. It's my belief that Toni will never go back to him now—there'll be a divorce whether Nat lives or dies."

"Let's go to sleep, sweetie, I've got a day's work ahead of me," grumbled Joe.

"Typical husband—all for the office—" she grumbled back.

They slept—loving, devoted and secure.

But not for long.

About five o'clock in the morning, the telephone rang. Chris got out of bed to answer it. The next moment she was in Toni's room, shaking her awake.

"Toni—Toni—you're wanted at the hospital."

Toni, drowsy from the effects of her deep sleep, took a few seconds to realise what was happening. Then she was wide awake and out of bed.

"What do they say? Is he dying?"

"Oh, darling, I don't know," said Chris, her face creased with anxiety for her friend, "I just don't know, but they want you."

Toni gave her a look from her large unhappy eyes that Chris would never forget.

"He's dying," she said under her breath.

"Don't think the worst. We'll get dressed and I'll drive you."

*   *   *

At the hospital the Night-Sister took Toni to Nat's private room. There were two doctors with Mr. Olver. They were giving him oxygen. He hadn't recovered consciousness and his heart was giving anxiety.

The nurse whispered to Toni:

"Day Sister told me to phone you if we were worried."

"Thank you," Toni whispered back. Her feelings were numb at this moment. She was conscious only of that black shadow of utter disaster that was hanging over her head.

When she saw the oxygen tent, two white-coated doctors with stethoscopes on one side of Nat, and a nurse on the other, her own heart seemed to fail.

If he dies, I will too, she said the words to herself.

They wouldn't let her near him. She stood by helpless, watching, realising that they were fighting for his life.

The room seemed very bare. All the flowers had been removed.

Then suddenly Toni, concentrating feverishly on all that she could see of Nat's poor face, saw his eyes open.

Before she could restrain herself, she let out a cry:

"Nat! *Nat!*"

Both physicians looked up sharply. The nurse turned round. But Toni only saw Nat. His eyes stayed open. She felt that it was a miracle, when his lips moved. Still more so, when the night Sister came across and said:

"Are you *Toni?*"

"Yes."

"He's asking for you."

"Is he going to die?" Toni asked stupidly. She felt stupified.

"No. His heart is already stronger. He's making an unexpected effort, and I'm sure if he sees you it'll help him still more, Mrs. Olver."

Toni didn't hear that name. She wouldn't have cared if she had heard it, nor corrected the nurse. She moved forward and knelt beside Nat's bed. She took one of his long inert hands—that strong right hand with the surgeon's spatulate fingers, which she had so often kissed. She kissed it now and in an anguish of emotion—of the most exquisite relief—whispered:

"Nat, Nat, my darling. Oh, Nat. . ."

His eyes closed, but opened again. He gave her the faintest smile, but it was a smile of recognition. She realised that he didn't know why she was here, and was much too ill to let that worry him. But she could see that his relief was as profound as hers. He spoke to her:

"Toni. . . darling. . ."

Then his eyelids closed again.

Still holding on to his hand, Toni looked up at one of the doctors.

"Is he all right? Will he be all right now?"

The young man, his fingers still around Mr. Olver's wrist, gave her a reassuring smile. Ye gods and little fishes, he thought, what a smashing-looking girl. Was this the great Mr. Olver's wife? He supposed so. Aloud he said:

"He'll do fine now. I suggest you go and wait comfortably in Sister's room. I'll call you again, perhaps in an hour or two's time."

Once more Toni kissed Nat's hand. She left it drenched with her tears.

*   *   *

In the waiting room she sobbed in Chris's arms, but this time, with wild relief and happiness.

"He's going to be all right. *He's going to be all right*. He knew me. He's out of danger. Oh, Chris, *Chris*, he's going to be all right!"

181

"Nobody," said Chris, with a long sigh, "could be more glad than I am!"

Three days later things looked still better. Once having turned the corner, Nat's natural resilience and vigour pulled him clean out of the shadows. There came the moment when he was able to sit up, propped by pillows, hold Toni's hand, and talk to her as animatedly as though he had never been the victim of an accident.

"The head's healing up nicely. Now there's talk of moving me to the old Queenbury. They need the private room here badly. I've no right to hold it up. Besides I'd like to be with the chaps I know—not that I don't appreciate all they've done for me here—they've been great."

Toni looked at him with deep love and satisfaction. His eyes were so blue and bright.

"Hurry up and get rid of those plasters on your face, they wreck your beauty," she said.

He grinned.

"If it's only my beauty you love me for I shall put an end to our affair."

She lifted his hand to her lips.

"Don't do that, darling. Our affair is really only just about to begin and I want it to go on and on and on until we die."

"Dear dramatic little Toni," he said, and in turn took her hand and kissed it, "I really don't think there's another girl like you in the world. They certainly don't grow on trees."

She lit a cigarette for him. He was allowed to smoke now. She talked to him seriously. It was the first time she had told the complete story of her departure from Guy and Rio.

"I think Guy really was dumbfounded when he saw me all ready to quit. But he couldn't stop me—no-one could. I thought I was going to lose you. I had to be with you. Oh, Nat, Nat, I went through some ghastly moments on that terrible flight home."

"Darling, it was superb of you to come. You're a brave little thing. It was a tremendous step to take."

"It wasn't. Nothing else mattered. The worst time for me was when I first left you and went back to Guy."

Nat looked at the point of his cigarette.

"I'd rather not be reminded of that. It was hell for me."

"Oh, darling," she said in a choked voice, "I hated going—terribly! But when I realised what Guy had cooked up—that infamous false testimony from Miss Withers—I just couldn't let it go on, now could I? Would you have stuck to me if you had known it was going to wreck all I'd ever built up and cherished most?"

Silence. Then Nat said:

"I suppose not. But I wanted you, too, Toni. Do you know, that wretched Teresa had the nerve to ring me up a few days before my accident and ask for a reference. Before I could refuse—which she anticipated—she began to whine about having been let down by someone who had promised her money, etc., etc. As though I didn't know the whole sordid story."

"How fantastic! But I suppose she was egged on by her boy-friend. He seems to have been a low type."

"And I presume that Guy had to part with quite a bit of money in his effort to knock me out. Little doubt he paid a handsome deposit to those two."

Toni drew away from Nat, stood up and began to rearrange the roses in one of the vases opposite him.

"And now we've got to readjust our lives," she said anxiously. "What do you suggest we do, Nat?"

"I don't care as long as you swear you won't walk out on me again."

She turned to him, starry-eyed.

"Never again. Oh, I swear it. Guy can't repeat his villainy and I won't leave you ever again."

"The divorce must go through."

She gave him another worried look.

"There'll still be a scandal for you, and there's Lord Sydell and all."

"Darling, I've *had* it so far as all that worrying and bothering is concerned. Let Guy get on with the divorce now. You're not to live alone—you're to live with me. I'm going to see Cousin Mervyn this afternoon. I shall arrange for him to take over my share of the lease and live with another chap. He's so often at sea, he won't mind. I shall take you home as soon as it's possible."

Toni's remarkable eyes suddenly shone. She sat on the edge of the bed and took both his hands, pressing them tightly.

"Oh, Nat, I begin to feel really alive and happy again. Oh, Nat, where shall we make our permanent home?"

"You can start looking for a cottage. I shall commute. Let's find something outside London, anyhow, where we can get away from Harley Street and everybody we know. Sussex—Surrey—wherever you like. Would you like that?"

"I'd adore it!" she said under her breath.

"Then it's as good as fixed."

"Meanwhile until you are better, Chris insists I stay with her. She and Joe really are the most fabulous friends."

"I'm in debt to them for a life-time," he said.

"And now," she said, "I'm going to leave you because Sister said you weren't to get tired, and I'm going home to write to Guy and ask him to divorce me as soon as he possibly can."

"And if he refuses?"

"Then I shall live with you," said Toni.

18

The letter that Toni wrote to her husband remained unanswered for at least three weeks.

At first Toni was worried. She knew Guy. She was not too happy about the delay or the situation in general. She wondered whether or not he was scheming something new and evil in order to be revenged upon Nat and herself.

For the moment, anyhow, she was too busy to find much time for thinking. First of all Nat was taken by ambulance to the Queenbury. There, in his own beloved hospital, he was looked after by colleagues and nurses who were old friends, and finally discharged with nothing more than a few strips of plaster on face and head to remind him that he had so nearly died.

Whatever might happen in the future, Keith Lucas-Wright showed the greatest friendliness all the time that Nat was laid up. As Nat remarked to Toni, Keith seemed quite ignorant of the reason Teresa Withers had so suddenly made her exit. Neither, so it would seem, had any news of Nat's misdeeds reached the ears of Sydell or the Board of Governors.

Nat was able finally to return to his flat the month after his accident. Toni insisted on going with him. Mervyn, for the second time since he started his leave, was away with friends in Scotland.

"My little sister might just as well come and look after me," Nat told Toni, jokingly.

But at the end of this month of silence from Guy, Toni began to panic. She wondered what he was up to. She felt no confidence nor could she even start to look for her dream cottage until she knew whether or not Guy intended to give her a divorce.

On further reflection, she decided that it was all very well to have told Nat that she would just live with him if she couldn't marry him. Perhaps she would! But even as things were today, it might be tricky for a medical man. They were both aware of this. Once again Toni moved back to Ovington Gardens. This time to please Joe who wanted to take his Chris away and leave Toni to look after the flat and the young nurse-maid Chris had found for her baby. But that was only for a fortnight, then the Masters came home. And then fate had a staggering surprise in store for Toni.

Guy answered her letter.

It was addressed to her c/o Mrs. Masters, the only address which he knew would be sure of finding her. Toni opened the letter feeling apprehensive but as she read it, her whole body began to throb with excitement. It was so unexpected and so utterly marvellous.

"My dear Antonia,

When you walked out on me for the second time I felt stunned as well as furiously angry. Then I calmed down and faced a few facts amongst which was the undeniable truth that we were and always had been totally unsuited. Also that I was a fool when I first met you in Paris to imagine that you would ever make the kind of wife or companion I wanted.

Most of our incompatibility may have been my fault. I still think you're a little fool but I'm sure you did your best and that I have been very difficult. An impossible husband for you. You are far too sentimental and your tastes too simple. It could never have worked. As for my wish to defeat you—that was an obsession which no longer exists. I still feel outraged by your conduct but since you went away something has happened to alter my whole life—even my way of thinking; I no longer wish to be revenged on either you or your lover.

Almost immediately after your departure, I received a telephone call from the widow of a Brazilian friend—Senhor Dalmahlo. Consuela had only just returned from America and heard that I was in Rio. She particularly wished to see me and asked us to dine with her at a private party in her apartment. Her husband who died a year ago was one of the richest men in Brazil. He made a fortune out of diamonds. I knew him well—originally a business contact—and remembered her as a strikingly attractive young woman in her thirties. When I told her you had returned to England she insisted I joined her party. I decided to go rather than be alone. During that evening Consuela and I found much in common. I had admired her greatly in the past and although she's a few years older than myself, she looks young, marvellously beautiful and exquisitely dressed. A polished woman of the world—the reverse of yourself, Antonia.

I admit that I poured out my sorrows to her and told her that our marriage had been a failure.

She was most sympathetic—more particularly she understood everything. She admitted that she had been no more suited to her late husband than I was to you.

I decided to prolong my stay in Rio especially to see Consuela. We spent every available moment together; she opened up the dazzling prospects of a new love and a new world.

Money is no object with either of us. As a pair financially, we realised we could rule an empire. I found her hypnotic and I seemed to appeal to her physically, mentally, in all ways.

She has none of your romanticism and much of my own peculiar type of sensuality. In other words—I became aware that I no longer wished to hold on to you and that my happiness lay with Consuela and she felt exactly the same about me.

It was what might be called 'a lightning affair' but more than that, we want to remain together. She is a Catholic but gave up her religion years ago and does not care in the least how I secure my divorce.

We intend to live in the Bahamas where she owns a superb property, and I shall take an apartment in New York. I can enjoy there all the expression of art and joy of collecting art treasures that I could wish for, in Consuela's company. She is a connoisseur. I shall make arrangements to leave London for good and am shortly joining Consuela in Nassau. We shall live there until we are able to marry. This, I hope, will be in the shortest possible time. I have written to my solicitors and given them instructions. You can divorce me. It will be speedier and less complicated done this way.

No doubt this decision will come as a pleasant surprise to you.

It may also surprise you to know that I do in my own queer fashion regret having caused you so much suffering, and in particular that I went to such crazy lengths to keep you with me. It was a madness I now deplore. We can make many mistakes in this world. But this time I am making no mistake. My marriage to Consuela will be satisfactory in every way.

So this time it really is good-bye, Antonia. I hope you will be happy with your doctor. Please do keep all your clothes and furs etc. which are still in the penthouse. Take them away. Let them be my wedding-present to you. And now good-bye. We are unlikely to meet again."

* * *

When Toni stopped reading this letter she felt almost suffocated with excitement. It was such an unexpected turn of events—it was hardly credible, including Guy's expression of regret for what he had done to her. On the other hand, she was not altogether surprised about the millionaire's widow.

She could see that a rich, polished soignée woman of the world might well make the right wife for a man like Guy. She, Toni, had been the wrong choice. She could even understand Consuela wanting Guy. The tall golden-haired, dignified Englishman, no matter how coldly vicious, would appeal to her. He was obviously her type. They would be a powerful combination.

So this meant that Nat was not going to be cited as a co-respondent now. Nothing, nothing, would blur the pages of his history at the hospital. That was the thing that delighted Toni most.

"Maybe we don't deserve to have things all our own way," she remarked to Chris after her friend had also read Guy's extraordinary letter. "What do you think?"

"I don't agree at all," said Chris, always stoutly loyal. "You would never have been unfaithful to Guy if he hadn't been such a so-and-so to you. Let him give you the divorce and be rid of him. I wish his wealthy widow joy."

"Oh, Chris, what a burden off our backs!" Toni exclaimed "Just imagine how marvellous it is for me to know that I haven't hurt Nat at all."

Chris rolled her eyes heavenwards.

"When will you ever stop thinking about Nat—and never of yourself?"

"From this moment onward I shall begin to think of myself," said Toni breathlessly, "I shall look for our cottage. I shall prepare for my own marriage, and I shall walk around with the most stupid look of content on my face, and everybody else will be fed up with me."

"And what about all the wonderful clothes and furs in the penthouse Guy mentioned?"

"They can stay there," said Toni promptly. "I shall thank Guy but I just don't want *anything* that can remind me of him, or our marriage. . ."

Chris suddenly giggled and gave her friend a pleading look.

"Oh, *please* don't get rid of the mink, Toni, it is so smart and does suit you so well."

"Okay," said Toni, "I won't get rid of the mink!" Then she added: "Forgive me, darling, if I don't stay and have that sandwich with you, I just must go and see Nat."

Nat had all but recovered from his accident with little more than a small scar or two to show, and an occasional bout of headaches which were growing less noticeable every day.

Today Nat had gone to the Royal Queenbury. He had stayed away from the place long enough, he told Toni, and he wanted to catch up with a lot of hospital 'gossip' and make arrangements for his return to work—in a week's time. He had had to abandon the private practice for the moment, but hoped to return to that in a few weeks. But he had been warned to go easy and he was sensible enough to obey orders.

When Toni gave Nat the letter from Guy, she said breathlessly:

"Miracles do happen, darling, they do. *They do.* Read this—"

"What on earth—?" he began.

"Read it," she repeated, "I'll make us some coffee. You look tired."

Even if he looked tired, Nat no longer felt it once he had got through that fantastic letter. He admitted that he was flabbergasted.

"*Guy*—wanting to get married again. *Guy*—willing to give you a divorce. It's incredible."

Toni's golden eyes sparkled.

"And see what it means. We'll be able to get married very soon and with the least possible fuss and nothing, no-one, can hurt you any more."

"Or you," he said and folded his arms around her and held her very close. "You've been absolutely marvellous to me all through. I don't know how I'm ever going to show you how grateful I am to you, Toni."

She pressed her cheek against his shoulder.

"Just go on loving me."

"That's easy."

"And take me to *Mas Candille* again. Let's spend our honeymoon in Mougins, shall we?"

"There's nothing I'd like better."

She looked around the room.

"And you'll give this up and we'll have our special cottage and garden and you'll become more and more famous as a surgeon and I'll make you a wonderful wife, I promise."

"You're a wonderful wife already," he said, "and it seems as though our luck's turned and the ending's going to be a happy one after all."

"They say happy endings are corny," Toni sighed, "and that great loves are always tragic."

"Nonsense," he grinned at her and kissed her on the tip of the nose. "We're turning our backs on tragedy. We're going to spend a wonderful afternoon making our plans for the future. You can write to that completely incomprehensible husband of yours, thank him for his letter, and say you'll put the whole thing into the hands of your solicitors immediately."

"How long do you think it will be before I'm free?"

"Oh, a few months. We'll try and hurry it up. Obviously Guy wants his freedom at once."

Toni disengaged herself from Nat's embrace but kept hold of both his hands as though fearing to let him go.

"Think of our room in *Mas Candille*, and the vapour floating out of that little green spiral candle—chasing away the mosquitoes. The smell of cedar wood and polish, and the red carnations, and outside, that wonderful valley; the mountains, and the twinkling lights. And our heavenly meals on the terrace. Oh, Nat, we'll have to explain to Mr. Bergman that our real name is Olver. There won't be a Mr. and Mrs. Gray *this time*.

"Oh, my Toni," he said, "you bring Mougins right into this room, darling—I feel I'm there already. Let's have a cigarette and drink our coffee and think about it some more."

Suddenly she said:

"Do you know, Nat, I don't envy that Senhora Consuela— not one little bit."

"Darling, she may suit Guy. You don't know. I believe every human being has his or her opposite number. You and Guy were as far removed from each other as you could possibly be."

"But *we* aren't, are we, Nat?"

"No—we aren't," he said and looked down into the golden shining eyes with great tenderness. "We're close, close together. And we're going to stay that way."